Scary Stories To Tingle Your Butt

7 Tales Of Gay Terror

CHUCK TINGLE

ISBN: 1517109965
ISBN-13: 978-1517109967

When your wife's ghost is in the closet talking like marbles and calling your name, don't answer her. This is a ghost trick and not safe. Stick to the spooky stories, goofball.

- Chuck Tingle

CONTENTS

ACKNOWLEDGMENTS

Thank you to all men that haunt butts, you are the real soul of scary books.

No thanks to Ted Cobbler, a snake in the grass who is scared of everything, even kid movies rated PG and PG-13.

1 BIGFOOT PIRATES HAUNT MY BALLS

I remember a time when the idea of pirates seemed silly and childlike. Where criminals of the sea were firmly relegated to the world of Hollywood blockbusters and amusement park rides. Birthday parties would be themed with skull and crossbones, a pirate's flag waving above chocolate cake and streamers.

I miss those days.

But things have changed, and now the very word pirate is enough to send a terrifying chill down the spine of any full grown man. It's a very different world, indeed.

The most ironic part of all of this, of course, is that the horror on the water began right here on the land. As humans, it was our fault, really; we should have known better than to continue our encroachment on the habitat of our bigfoot neighbors. But greed is a powerful thing, and soon the forests were being hacked to pieces while apartments and minimarts were erected in their place. Rivers were dammed and replaced with roads while black smog filled the sky above.

Many of the bigfeet assimilated into human culture, several of them becoming very successful and ushering in a new world of human/bigfoot relations. There were bigfoot doctors, bigfoot lawyers and even a bigfoot president who was incredibly well liked by the American people.

But not all of the bigfeet wanted to adapt to the civilized world of jobs and taxes, and our cities didn't slow down with their brutal swell into the wilderness.

Soon, these wild bigfeet had nowhere left to go but off into the vast oceans, leaving the forest in droves as they set out to sea on massive barges of lashed together tree trunks. We watched them go with a sense of relief, glad that these ultimate protectors of the wilderness had finally hoisted the white flag of surrender. Of course, we never could have expected what would happen when the bigfeet came back.

Soon, human vessels were being boarded left and right, cruise ships pillaged for supplies and oilrigs set on fire. The bigfoot pirates were ruthless seamen, environmental terrorists of the open waters with an axe to grind against the society that had cast them out of house and home.

Of all these fearsome bigfoot pirates however, one stood tall above the rest as the most cutthroat pirate of them all; Lorko the Black.

Lorko was a ferocious bigfoot from Dallas, Texas, who was said to have commandeered more vessels than every other bigfoot pirate combined. He ruled the seas with utter villainy as captain of his ship, Nice Abs, striking fear up and down the west coast and particularly the waters around Santa Monica, which is where I happen to live.

Encounters with Lorko were the stuff of legends around these parts, ranging from the time someone saw his massive pirate ship pass by in the early morning haze, to a near death battle in which the storyteller barely escaped with their life.

This is why it was such a huge deal when the Nice Abs was finally sunk just a few miles off the coastline, after a fearsome battle with the United States Navy.

The general reaction to the news was quite odd. On one hand, having such a violent criminal off the water was an absolute blessing, yet somehow the bigfoot pirate captain would be missed. Over time, Lorko had become a sort of celebrity around town, almost like a mascot for the city of Santa Monica. It didn't hurt that the bigfoot was incredibly handsome, a muscular creature with broad shoulders and a winning smile, but it was still hard for me personally to get behind celebrating a wanton criminal like he was some kind of folk hero.

That's not the only strange thing that started happening after Lorko died, however.

The first time I felt the ache in my balls I was taking my morning walk along the beach with my dog, Skippy. Skippy was playing in the waves, barking and dancing with jovial excitement as he fought against the ever changing tide. It was a day like any other, until suddenly I found myself buckling under the throbbing ache of a pain deep within my balls. I held fast, hunched over until the surges of discomfort passed completely, but by the time it was over I knew that something was dreadfully wrong.

I immediately booked an appointment with my doctor, and no more than twenty four hours later I found myself sitting in his Santa Monica office, waiting for my test results.

The door to my private room opens and my doctor walks in with a clipboard in his hand, causing me to sit up abruptly.

"Andy." Dr. Torp says, a concerned look plastered across his face. "We've got your results."

"And?" I ask, on the edge of my seat. I have a variety of different illnesses in my family and a diagnosis of any one of them would be devastating. "Just give it to me straight, doc. How sick am I?"

Dr. Toro shakes his head. "Well, you're not sick, actually." He explains.

I stare at him blankly. "I'm not?" A smile of relief slowly begins to creep across my face.

"But don't get too excited." Dr. Torp tells me. "You're still in a world of trouble. I'm afraid your balls are haunted."

I freeze, hit suddenly with a wave of utter shock and anxiety. Of all the potential outcomes, I never would have guessed that this feeling within my balls was one of spiritual possession, but my doctor is a good one and I have no other choice but to trust his diagnosis.

“Haunted by who?” I ask, slowly, not exactly sure that I want to hear the answer.

Dr. Torp sits down in a chair across from me and shrugs. “At this point, we can’t say for sure, it’s too early in the haunting to get any real sense of who, or what, has possessed your balls. Eventually, though, the paranormal occurrences will become more and more frequent and you will likely be visited by some kind of apparition.”

“A ghost?” I ask.

Dr. Torp nods.

“From my balls?” I continue.

Dr. Torp nods again. “Once that happens you should listen very carefully to what this apparition has to say. A lot of the time these ball hauntings are caused when a spirit is not yet ready to move on from the material world, they have unfinished business to take care of and they’re not going to leave until they do. It could be anything from delivering a message to a loved one, to building a massive art museum; you just don't know."

I let out a sigh. "So you're telling me that I have to drop everything in *my* life and take care of whatever this ghost needs me to take care of?"

"I'm afraid so." Dr. Torp tells me. "Let's just hope that whoever is haunting your balls is reasonable with their request."

I'm laying in bed that night when the pain starts to flare up again, a throbbing ache from deep within my balls that causes me to toss and turn, eventually waking me from my slumber. I sit up in bed, the cool Santa Monica air floating through the window and tickling my skin with a pleasant freshness.

It takes my eyes a moment to adjust to the darkness, but when they do I jump suddenly, surprised by the appearance of a large, semi-transparent figure standing at the foot of my bed. I immediately recognize him.

"You're Lorko the Black." I stammer. "The most notorious bigfoot pirate to ever sail the seven seas."

"Aye." Says the towering bigfoot ghost with a nod.

In person, he is even more handsome than I expected, his muscular frame simultaneously imposing and arousing. He is covered head to toe in jet black fur, an eye patch fastened tightly around one eye while the other stares down at me with devilish intensity.

"Why are you haunting my balls?" I ask. "Why me?"

Lorko shakes his head. "I didn't choose this fate, matey, it's simply the one I was dealt."

For a moment I find myself deeply connected to this spectral bigfoot pirate. In many ways we are both in the same boat, thrust into a situation that neither of us asked for by the random hand of fate. Now we are connected by an unbreakable chain that stretches well beyond the realms of life and death, the haunter and the haunted woven together for reasons that we may never truly understand.

Beneath the sheets, my cock starts to grow, throbbing alongside my balls as I take in the powerful physique of this majestic bigfoot.

"What do you want from me?" I ask him. "I need you to stop haunting my balls. I mean, you seem like a nice guy but it really hurts."

"Aye, the cold grip of death is a bastard!" Agrees Lorko. "It was not my intent to make 'yer balls ache like two oysters in the deep."

"Then help me." I beg. "Help me help you. What is your unfinished business?"

Lorko sighs as I say this, sitting down at the edge of my bed as his entire demeanor changes from fearsome pirate to old friend. "Now that is a hell of a tale." The bigfoot pirate ghost tells me. "One that needs to stay between you and me."

I nod in understanding.

"Aye then, listen up." Lorko begins. "My crew and I may have been the most dreaded pirates in the whole sea, but we were also the most secretive. Most folk thought it was because we were plotting something devious, but the truth of the matter is that my crew and I…" Lorko trails off.

"What is it?" I beg to know. "You can tell me."

"The truth of the matter," Lorko begins again, "is that my crew and I are gay."

I gasp in astonishment, completely blindsided by this revelation. "Lorko the Black has been gay this whole time?" I ask. "That's amazing."

"Is it now?" Lorko chuckles.

"Well, yeah." I offer. "I mean there's nothing wrong with that. I'm gay, too."

Lorko eyes me up and down for a moment. "Well, that might explain why your balls are the ones being haunted."

"And why my cock is so hard?" I add, genuinely curious.

Lorko shakes his head. "I'm only haunting your balls, the shaft is all yours, mate."

I'm suddenly embarrassed by my careless admission, showing all of my cards right up front. This whole time I had thought my wanton attraction to the glorious bigfoot pirate was just part of the haunting, but now I realize that I truly am just incredibly turned on by the semi-transparent beast that stands before me.

"The thing is, me and my crew never had a chance to live out our gay lifestyle." Continues Lorko the Black. "We were adhering to the strict pirate code of no buggery, and had yet to find a civilian man who was willing to fulfill our desires as a gay crew. This is where you come in."

"Me?" I repeat, my heart pounding hard in my chest.

"Go down to the marina and take your boat out into the darkness of the night. There in the mist we'll find you."

"Right now?" I stammer.

Before I can even get the words out, however, Lorko is gone, disappearing into thin air right before my very eyes.

My balls still ache for release. I let out a long sigh and then climb out of bed. I put on my coat and get ready to head down to the marina.

The ocean around me is eerily still as I putt slowly out across the water in my small boat, not exactly sure where I should be going but scanning the darkness for sign. It's a beautiful night, clear as can be while I gaze up into the sky above of the twinkling lights of Santa Monica that drift farther and farther behind me. It's been too long since I've been out here on the ocean, and regardless of whether on not I find Lorko out here, I'm still glad that I came.

By now, I'm beginning to think that all of this might have been a mistake. The events of an hour earlier now seem like nothing more than a strange fever dream, a brief lapse into delusional fantasy thanks to the mounting stress of a serious medical haunting.

I'm just about to give up and turn around when suddenly I notice a strange light mist floating out across the water towards me. There is no reason for fog tonight, and when I look a little closer the wafting smoke seems to be of an ethereal nature. The mist grows thicker and thicker until suddenly I'm surrounded by a wall of white, the shore and the sky completely obscured from vision.

Suddenly, out of nowhere comes Lorko's massive pirate ship, emerging from the haze like a demon from hell. There are torches alight down either side of its deck, illuminating an entire crew of semi-translucent bigfoot pirates and their handsome captain Lorko. My balls throb with a haunted ache.

"Ahoy!" Shouts down Lorko the Black. "So glad you could make it, Andy."

The next thing I know, a ladder is tossed over the edge of the pirate ship and lowered down to me so that I can grab on. I quickly lash my boat to the side of Lorko's vessel and then climb up the ladder, eventually emerging over the edge of the deck.

The entire gang of bigfoot pirates cheer when they see me, excitedly exchanging glances with one another as I stand before them.

"Welcome to the Nice Abs!" Lorko tells me. "How are you balls?"

"Haunted." I tell him.

"Well worry not, matey." Lorko shouts. "Soon, your ass will be just as haunted as your balls."

I know that his words are meant to scare and intimidate me, but as I stand here before the ghostly bigfoot pirates, I find myself overwhelmed by a much more powerful sensation than fear; arousal.

"You can haunt every inch of my body." I tell the crew seductively. "I'm here to finish your business, your *gay* business."

Lorko laughs aloud and looks to the rest of his crew. "You heard him boys! Get to it!"

The next thing I know I'm dropping down to my knees as the bigfoot pirates begins to circle around me. The mythical beasts stand tall and proud, towering over me with their muscular, fur covered bodies while I look up at them with cock hungry eyes.

"Give me those ghost bigfoot dicks." I demand.

The crew knows what to do next, pulling out their thick furry cocks and pushing them towards me from every angle. I take one in each hand and start to stroke rapidly, beating them off as I wrap my mouth around Lorko's swollen rod.

He pushes forward and I try my best to take him, struggling slightly as his length forces its way past my gag reflex and into the depths of my neck. My eyes start to water as he pumps back and forth within me, moving in and out of my wet lips with firm, manly thrusts. Eventually, he pushes forward and holds, plunging as deep as he can go and making me choke on his cock. I make a strange, tortured gurgle as my face comes to rest against the captain's hard, bigfoot abs, my eyes bulging until he pulls back and releases me.

As his cock retracts from my mouth I find myself gasping for air, sputtering and spitting as I desperately look from one pirate to the next with wild eyes.

"Tell me what you want to do to me!" I beg them. "Call me your dirty human twink!"

The bigfoot pirates exchange glances, clearly thrilled about the total freak whose balls they've been haunting.

"You like that undead sasquatch dick you fucking human sissy?" Lorko the Black asks me. "You like being haunted in your balls by a bigfoot poltergeist while you suck me off?"

I start to answer but the words are cut off as he shoves his thickness into my mouth, then processes to slam my head down again and again onto his member. His massive hairy hands behind my head, I struggle against him until finally he releases and passes me on to someone else. This continues until the whole ship has had a turn at fucking my face and the tears run down my cheeks.

"More." I groan. "I need more ghost dick."

"Stand the fuck up." Lorko commands, pulling me to my feet.

He spins me around, roughly, and then pulls off my pants, then boxer briefs, and throws them to the side. I balance myself with both hands against the railing of the pirate ship, poking my bare ass out towards them while I gaze across the black water before me.

"Take my living human ass." I tell the crew, locking my knees and bending forward.

The guys do as they're told, lining up one by one behind me with Lorko at the front. He takes his time, aligning his cock with my tight hole and then he pushes forward, causing me to jump in shock from the foreign sensation. I feel my ass opening up, the rim of it stretching to accommodate the ghost captain's enormous bigfoot dick. I let out a long, loud moan of pleasure and pain, reeling from the unfamiliar sensation as Lorko the Black begins to slowly pump in and out of me. Lorko grasps my hips tightly for a better angle and then continues to plow, entering me fully before pulling back and throwing in a few hard slap of his hand against my ass cheek for good measure.

"Fuck him good, captain!" One of the crew chimes in, a catcall that's greeted with uproarious cheers from the others. "Take that human butthole to town!"

Lorko's slamming me hard now as I look back at him with pleading eyes. My cock is rock hard, so I reach down and start to stroke off my shaft while he pummels me.

After a while, Lorko tags himself out and lets one of his crew have a go. This bigfoot is somehow even bigger than Lorko was, and when he pushes inside of me I can't help but scream out into the darkness. It doesn't stop him for one second, though, and moments later I'm getting pounded again as I bite my lip and take it like the bad, bad boy that I am.

Once again the beasts cycle through, using my asshole like their own personal gay sex toy. The gang's rough treatment of my muscular body makes me insanely horny, and it's not long before I find myself right on the edge of blowing a massive load. I'm just about there when Lorko grabs me and pulls me away from the railing.

"Where are we going?" I ask.

Lorko lies right down onto the wooden deck, his firm cock jutting out from his ripped body.

"Get over here." He tells me. I walk over to him and Lorko motions for me to spin around, which I do, then he commands for me to squat down onto his thickness.

I lower myself slowly, dropping until I feel the tip of his shaft knock against my backdoor. I take a deep breath, relaxing as much as I can before letting myself fall all the way, then leaning back as his massive spectral shaft enters me and throwing my legs out in the air to either side. Lorko pulls me against him, my back pressed down onto his furry, chiseled chest, and then he begins to pump in and out of my butthole.

One of the other majestic undead bigfeet climbs down in front of me and positions himself on his knees. His cock engorged and ready, the creature aligns himself with my already taken ass and then pushes forward, entering me simultaneously with the shaft that's already pounding my tightness from beneath. Having never been double penetrated before; I hardly know what to do with myself.

I buck forward and back as the two monsters thrust into my body in tandem with one another. The bigfeet work in perfect synchronicity, causing me to tremble with wave after wave of intense, blissful sensation.

"Are you a bad little twink human?" One of them asks me.

"I'm am." I say, my voice quivering with every hard thrust.

"Do you like taking those two bigfoot ghost dicks?" Lorko demands to know, grabbing my ass cheeks and spreading me out from below while the two of them slam into my taut asshole. I'm stretched wide around them, barely able to accommodate their immense size.

"I love taking bigfoot ghost dicks!" I scream. "Haunt my asshole like you haunt my fucking balls!"

Suddenly, there is a bigfoot pirate ghost standing at either side of me and one in the front, straddling my face. I quickly grab the beasts to the left and right and begin to furiously beat their long hairy shafts. The bigfoot who has stepped in front of me takes me by the head and pushes his cock deep down my throat, gagging me.

Now, my hands full of cock while two monsters pound my ass and another takes my throat, I truly feel like the filthy gay twink that I am; and I absolutely love it.

This whole time I thought I was helping the ghostly crew come to terms with their death, but now I realize that they've helped me come to terms with my life as a cock hungry bigfoot lover.

As a human encroaching on the land of these majestic bigfeet, I'd gotten so used to having everything handed to me. Now, actually being out here on the dark water and taking what I want from the world is utterly refreshing.

The pirates continue to pound me with their fat furry cocks, and as they do I find that familiar sensation of prostate orgasm creeping back across my body. It feels nice and warm, tingling as it travels from my dick to my stomach and then down across my arms and legs in a lustful fire. I start to shake, my eyes rolling back into my head and my legs kicking out straight while the sensation finally overtakes me and I explode from within. My dick begins ejecting hot cum everywhere in a series of forceful pumps.

"Oh my god!" I scream, my voice muffled by the dick in my throat.

The bigfeet don't let up for a second, slamming into my with everything that they've got as I convulse and spasm between them in ecstasy. I grab tightly onto the creature in front of me, hanging on for dear life as I howl and scream and then finally I fall back between them, fucked silly.

The monsters inside of my asshole are quick to follow, letting out groans of their own as they blow their hot white loads up inside of me. I can feel the semen fill my body, bursting out around the edge of their cocks and running down my ass crack and legs in thick, messy streaks. As they slide of out me, a torrent of ghost jizz comes flowing out as well, spilling onto the deck below.

The rest of the crew stand and beat their cocks, anxious to blow across my face. I stick out my tongue playfully and look upward, coaxing them along as I play with their hanging bigfoot balls.

Moments later, they start to explode.

The first one shoots a warm rope of semen across my mouth, running from cheek to cheek like a liquid smile. I laugh a little and turn to the next beast, who blasts an utterly enormous load onto my pink tongue. I swallow hungrily as the final two step up on either side of me and quickly finish off in similar fashion, painting my face with even more streaks of milky white. I'm completely plastered with cum.

I lay back onto the hard wood below, exhausted; catching my breath until finally the bigfeet help me up.

"That was fantastic!" Yells Lorko the Black, clapping his hands together. "Thanks for helping us out there. I think it's safe to say that our business as ghost pirates is now finished!"

The whole crew cheers and I smile with warm enthusiasm.

"Time to celebrate!" Shouts the captain. "And what would a celebration be without someone walking the plank?"

Again the crew cheers, and I cheer with them until suddenly I feel myself being grabbed by the arms and roughly hoisted into the air.

"Wait!" I scream. "Me? What are you doing?"

"Sorry, mate!" Lorko calls out as the rest of the pirates carry me over to the edge. "We don't have a plank so it looks like we'll just have to throw you overboard. Never trust a pirate, and especially not a bigfoot pirate ghost!"

"No!" I cry, but it's too late. Suddenly, I flying through the air, tossed overboard by the crew and plummeting down towards the cold, dark water below.

I sit up with a gasp. This time, instead of my bedroom, I find myself surrounded by the beautiful Santa Monica coastline as the sun rises behind me, casting the sand with a beautiful, golden hue. I'm soaking wet, but alive.

Lying in the sand next to me is a note in a bottle, which presumably washed up onto the shore at about the same time. I grab the bottle and pop off the cork, removing the curled parchment from within.

I unfurl the paper and read aloud.

"Dear Andy." The page says, the words written in a beautiful inked script. "Sorry to scare you like that, but us pirates have a difficult time with goodbyes. Sometimes it's easier to just throw someone overboard than having to tell them the truth."

My heart is suddenly pounding, tears welling up in my eyes as I read the words before me. I don't want to read anymore because I know what it's about to say, and I just don't know if my heart can take it.

"The truth is," I finally continue reading, "I love you."

I crumble forward in the sand, overwhelmed by emotions. I had only just met this bigfoot pirate ghost and gangbanged his crew, but in this short time I had also fallen hard for the spectral sasquatch. Now, however, he is gone.

When I finally get up the courage I continue to read aloud through the tears. "Just know that we will be together again someday in the afterlife." Torko writes.

My balls no longer ache, the haunting gone from their delicate hang.

I put the note back into the bottle and then stand up, looking out across the water as the sun continues to rise. I have faith that one day I well see my captain again, like a bird returns in the springtime or a man returns to the frozen lake of his wife's drowning year after year. One day, I will see Torko again. One day, he will haunt more than just my balls.

2 VAMPIRE NIGHT BUS POUNDS MY BUTT

Public transportation can be a real pain in the ass, especially when you're used to getting around with your very own car, and on your very own schedule.

Even though the traffic in Los Angeles is mind numbingly bad, there is a certain Zen-like quality to sitting behind the wheel and working your way through an hour-long podcast in your own bumper-to-bumper cage on wheels. It's a great place to think or even just sing loudly, drumming your hands on the dashboard with the pleasant assurance that no one else will ever hear you.

I was one of those happy commuters until just last week, when I was sideswiped off the road by a truck and trailer in a hit and run that, apparently, doesn't mean much to the Los Angeles Police Department.

Now I'm just waiting for my insurance company to come through with some sort of compensation, and in the meantime I've been taking the bus too and from work.

One things for sure about public transportation though, you meet a lot of strange people when you're hitting the evening routes. The city of angels is already full of weirdos, but the dark side of this town really starts to show itself as soon as the sun finally disappears beneath the shimmering blue ocean, casting the landscape in an endless shadow of strangeness until morning.

It was on one of these nights that I first heard about the Vlad.

I had just boarded and taken my seat near the back of the bus, when another rider climbed aboard and shuffled over next to me. He was strange and old, seemingly homeless but not as dirty as you would expect, just odd in his mannerisms.

"Nice night." The man says, sitting down a few rows in front of me on the vacant bus and then spinning around to talk back over the seat.

"Yeah, it is." I respond, trying not to do anything that would make him any more interested in me then he already is, yet still having the decency to be polite and answer the man's question. I continue to stare out from the bus window as the city rumbles by us on the other side of the glass.

"You've been riding this line a lot, huh?" Continues the man, curiously. "I've seen you."

At this point, I finally look at the guy and make eye contact, taking him in completely. He seems harmless enough, just strange.

"Yeah, I thought I recognized you." I tell the man.

Suddenly, the guy stands up and moves two rows back towards me, immediately sitting down in the seat next to mine on an almost completely empty bus. I'm instantly uncomfortable.

"I'm gonna tell you this because I like you." The man says. "Make sure you double check the bus you're getting on at this stop."

"Oh yeah?" I ask, my curiously piqued despite the blatant invasion of my personal space.

The strange man nods. "This is Vlad's route, too. If you're not careful you might end up turned into a bat, or even stone cold dead."

Despite my best efforts, a mischievous grin crosses my face. I had given him the benefit of the doubt at first, but now it has become painfully clear that, like most of the other disheveled looking folks boarding the bus at this late hour, he is utterly insane. At least he's making my commute a little more entertaining than usual

"Who's Vlad?" I ask, playing along.

"Bus thirteen." The man replies, staring at me with a deep and feverish intensity.

"Vlad drives thirteen?" I question.

"No, no." The man shakes his head. "Vlad *is* bus thirteen."

Suddenly, I realize what this strange man is talking about. Most of the Los Angeles city busses have assigned drivers, many of which I have recently come to know quite well, but others are driven by the sentient busses themselves. These living vehicles are rare but not unheard of, and my scoffing at one could be seen by some as racially insensitive. Living busses have had to fight to get where they are today, and that struggle is nothing to make light of.

Something still doesn't make sense, though.

"What do you mean turned into a bat?" I continue my line of questioning.

The man leans in, lowering his voice down to a hushed whisper. "Bus thirteen is a vampire."

I scoff loudly, unable to help myself as the mysterious man's absurd words cross my ears. Of course he thinks the living night bus is a vampire, this is exactly the type of racially insensitive thinking that has kept these sentient vehicles in the position that they're in, working minimum wage jobs without any real way to pull themselves out of the lower class. Stories like this one may seem like nothing but a little harmless fun, but when you realize the subconscious place of misdirected fear that they are coming from, the whole idea starts to put a bad taste in your mouth.

The mysterious man can see now that he's clearly lost me, and a look of great disappointment sweeps across his face. "You don't believe me, huh?" He asks.

I shake my head. "I'm sorry, no, and I think it's very insensitive to talk about living busses that way."

Our vehicle soon pulls over and the strange man almost immediately stands up, heading for the door and then climbing off onto the darkened street. As the bus pulls away he takes one final glance back at me, his expression not one of anger or frustration, but sadness, as if he knows a terrible fate that waits for me just around the next corner of my life.

I lean back into my seat and put on my headphones, anxious to get home.

By the next night I've completely forgotten about my bizarre warning from the evening before, my thoughts consumed instead by an aching frustration with my job and the fact that I had to work much later than I expected. Now, my schedule has been completely turned upside down, the usual bus route home a thing of the past. Instead, I've been thrust into a web of late night transit maps that I don't completely understand, especially after my brain has been fried from a long day at the office.

I arrive to my usual bus stop at this unusual time, scrolling through my phones transit app in complete, bewildered confusion. Nothing seems to make any sense until it suddenly hits me, I've already missed the last bus home but only a few minutes.

"Oh fuck." I say out loud, thinking back to the offer that my coworker had just made to drive me home. I had immediately turned him down out of sheer pride, wanting to show the world, and myself, that I can make it work and back in this big, bad city without a car of my own. I'm immediately regretting that decision.

The streets around me are completely empty, void of the daytime hustle and bustle the usually accompanies this part of town.

I let out a long sigh as I realize that I'll have to call a cab, which means the trip home will probably cost me just about half of the day's earnings at work. What a fucking disaster.

I'm just about to press enter on my cell phone to call the nearest cabby when I hear a low and familiar rumble in the distance. I look up immediately, a wave of relief washing over me as I see a lone night bus rumbling down the street. I'm thankful for his arrival until the bus gets close enough for me to make out the number flashing digitally across his forehead, thirteen.

The bus pulls up in front of me and stops, the doors opening to reveal not a single living soul inside, not even a driver.

"Where are you headed?" This bus asks in a thick, Eastern European accent.

I gulp hard. "North Hollywood."

"You're in luck." The bus retorts. "That's exactly where I'm headed."

"What are the chances?" I say aloud, almost to myself as I climb aboard. The warnings from the night before suddenly come flooding back over me as a long, cold chill runs down my spine.

The bus begins to roll onward as I take a seat next to the window, gazing out upon the darkened city streets that pass us by.

As ridiculous as it is to believe in vampires, the bus himself had all of the features that you'd normally associate with such devilish creatures of the night. The accent was obvious, but the vehicle was also incredibly handsome in a dark and brooding kind of way, with huge dark eyes and a muscular chest, with abs just barely visible underneath his large metallic frame.

My entire body is wracked with nervous tension now as I sit in silence, my thoughts flooded with by fearsome cocktail of emotion. In my mind, I just keep repeating to myself over and over again that vampires are not real, trying in vain to calm down. It's no use.

Suddenly, the bus speaks up, causing me to jump abruptly in my seat. "What are you doing out this late?"

"Oh, me?" I stammer, the phrase made even more awkward by the fact that there is nobody else on the bus with me. "They kept me for a really long time at work."

"That is most unfortunate." The vehicle responds me, his voice deep and velvety.

We sit in silence for a brief moment that, somehow, seems to stretch on forever and ever between us.

"You are nervous." The bus finally says, the statement ringing out like a question despite the fact that he never actually asked one.

"Yes." I say, my voice trembling now.

"Why?" The bus asks.

I think hard about how I want to answer, and then finally respond to his question with a question of my own. "Do you have any day routes?"

The bus smirks. "I spend my days asleep in a garage at my home, I only come out for the night shifts."

"Sure." I nod. "But don't you sometimes need a tune up during the day or anything like that?"

The bus shakes his head. "No, never."

"Interesting." I tell him, thinking hard about any other tests I could throw out there. "Are there any church services on this route?"

"It's a little late for that." The bus laughs. "Why do you ask?"

In reality, I'm just wondering how often folks wearing crosses ride this bus, but I can't tell him that so instead I offer a simple, "Just curious."

"You have some odd questions." The bus tells me.

I nod and then lean back into my seat, focusing once again on the darkened city that passes by out the window.

It suddenly dawns on me that we are no longer headed towards my North Hollywood destination, instead making our way up into the hills, farther and father away from the densely populated areas of Los Angeles. My heart immediate starts to pound hard in my chest.

"Where are we going?" I ask. "This isn't the way."

"I thought I'd take the scenic route." The bus tells me. "If you'd like

I can turn around and get you there quicker, but I thought you might enjoy a nice drive with me."

His words should come of as menacing, but instead there is a hint of something deeper and almost charming about his tone. I find myself intrigued by the vehicle's proposition and, dare I say, strangely aroused.

"It's fine." I tell him. "Let's take the long way."

I realize now that my cock is growing hard within my pants, unable to escape the strange charisma of his handsome city vehicle. It's an odd feeling, and at first I try to fight it as I recall the dread that had so fully consumed me just moments before. Regardless of how hard I try, though, my thoughts continue to return again and again to ones of decadent sexual attraction for this city vehicle.

As the minutes tick by, we travel farther and farther away from the lights of Los Angeles, up and down the hill and then out towards the edge of the deep valley. We are clearly no longer taking the long way home, but I don't mention it.

There's a part of me that's utterly terrified, yes, but at this point there's really nothing that I can do aside from jumping from the bus while it moves and potentially hurting myself badly. Not only that, but the fear that simmers inside of me is kind of arousing in itself.

"I know you're not taking me back to my house." I finally tell the bus, my voice trembling.

"Where am I taking you then?" The city bus replies.

"I don't know." I say. "Am I safe?"

"Yes, of course." The bus tells me. "You're my guest for the evening and you will be treated as such. Unless you'd like to go home now?"

I think about his offer for quite a while, and then finally respond with, "No, take me wherever you want."

"We're almost there." Says the bus.

Moments later, an incredible castle comes into view, with massive turrets and an spooky, gothic exterior. It looks as though it's been pulled straight from the screen of an old black and white horror film, yet it's located just a short drive outside of Los Angeles.

We pull in through the wrought iron gate and then cruise up to the front of the massive building, it's enormous double doors towering above us. I step out of the bus and crane my neck to look up at the castle's incredible stonework.

"Welcome." The bus says, opening the doors for me and revealing a giant entryway, which is large enough to fit the bus as he slowly wheels inside and closes the door behind us.

"Your home is beautiful." I tell him. "But you've invited me in without even introducing yourself."

"You know my name." The bus says in a powerful, deep tone.

"Vlad." I respond, a shiver consuming me as the word slips past my lips.

"Yes." The bus says. "And you are?"

"Rick." I tell him.

The bus nods. "Rick, you are my guest tonight at Castle Vlad, where all of your darkest fantasies will come true."

If anyone else would have said this to me I would have laughed out loud at the innate cheesiness of the line, but something about this city bus is so sincere, so passionate, that I don't dare make a peep. I once considered myself a typical straight male, but at this point I am utterly taken with the vehicle and his dark charms.

"Come with me" The bus says, continuing deeper into the house with a faint mechanical rumble.

The stairs of the castle have been remodeled since whenever they were built, now replaced by large stone ramps that are big enough for the vehicle to climb up and down with ease.

I follow Vlad to the upper landing where he stops in front of a beautiful fireplace that's inlaid with all kinds of stonework ghosts and goblins. There's a beautiful, red velvet chair next to the fireplace that Vlad motions for me to sit in, and I don't hesitate.

Almost immediately, the hearth erupts in a ball of glorious orange flame, lit spontaneously as if by some magical means. I can't help but gasp and pull away, but as the warmth begins to wash over me and the firelight shimmers across the stone walls, I settle in.

I'm finally relaxed enough to ask this beautiful bus something I've been dying to know ever since he picked me up.

"Tell me," I start, eyeing up the Los Angeles city vehicle curiously. "Are you a vampire?"

Vlad smiles, much wider now than any time previously, and reveals two massive fangs protruding from his upper gums. "What do you think?"

"Yes." I respond nervously. I quickly follow up. "Are you going to kill me? Or turn me into a bat?"

There is an awkward pause and then suddenly the large passenger vehicle bursts out laughing. "No, I'm not going to kill you. Of course not."

I let out a long sigh of relief.

"The blood drinking vampires of the past are long gone, slowly brought to extinction by their insistence of such a particular and rare diet." The bus explains. "I mean, I love blood, don't get me wrong, it's just hard to dine when you have to kill someone every time you're hungry."

"So what do you drink now?" I ask.

Vlad cracks a knowing grin. "Cum."

I was already hard before, but suddenly my arousal is kicked into overdrive.

"Have you ever been with a city bus?" Vlad asks, rolling towards me slowly.

"Once." I tell him. "In college."

"How about a vampire?" He asks, now so close to me that I can feel the heat of his engine radiating against my aching body.

"Never." I tell the vampire.

Suddenly, the arousal I feel for Vlad overtakes me completely. I tear off my shirt and then press myself against his warm bus body, kissing him hard.

"I want you." I tell the vampire vehicle, breathlessly. "I want to pleasure you like you deserve to be pleasured."

"Then do it." Says the bus with a cool confidence.

"Where's that fucking cock of yours?" I demand to know.

Vlad motions over his shoulder. "Inside."

There is a loud hiss as the doors open and I quickly climb aboard, walking back through the rows and rows of seats until I find it, a massive dick that projects proudly from the back wall of the bus.

"Fuck, you're so big!" I call out to him, wondering how I hadn't noticed this cock before.

"I know." Says the vampire bus.

I immediately drop down to my knees and get to work, taking his fat rod between my lips and then pumping my face up and down along Vlad's hard shaft. I can feel the bus shudder and tremble below me, clearly enjoying himself as I service him.

After a while of this I finally get up the courage to attempt a deep throat, taking a long breath and then pushing his cock as hard as I can against the back of my throat. Unfortunately, something deep within me just doesn't want to give way and moments later I come up for air with a loud gasp.

"Too much for you?" The bus laughs.

"Never." I tell him, trying once again but this time relaxing myself entirely. I push his dick lower and lower into me, his length sinking deep within my neck until finally it drifts past my gag reflex and hits bottom. My nose is now pressed hard against the metallic back wall of the vehicle, his balls hanging lightly against my chin while I hold him here.

Vlad let's out a long, satisfied moan, savoring the sensation of being completely consumed.

Finally, when I've just about ran out of air completely, I pull back with a loud gasp and let the giant rod pop out of my mouth. A strand of saliva runs from the head of his shaft to my lips, connecting the two of us together.

"You're cock is so fucking beautiful." I gush. "I've never been with another man, or bus, before, but I think I'm ready to take things even farther."

"I think you are, too." Vlad says.

I stand up and then quickly remove my pants, tossing them onto one of the seats as I spin around and back my bare, muscular ass up against the tip of his throbbing member. I tease the bus playfully, placing his huge dick right at the entrance of my butthole and allowing him to tease the rim.

I play with Vlad like this for a while until finally having mercy and pushing myself back onto his rod, which slips slowly inside of my butt. I let out an aching moan. My body is barely equipped to take his enormous size, but somehow I manage as my asshole stretches to its absolute limits. My entire being is flooded with a mixture of pain and pleasure, which transitions towards pure ecstasy with every pump that I make against Vlad's giant dick.

"How do you like that vampire bus cock?" Vlad demands to know, impaling me perfectly with his rock hard shaft. "Do you love that huge public transportation dick up your tight little asshole?"

"I love it!" I tell him. "I fucking love it!"

I'm hammering against his massive rod hard now, slamming the back wall of the bus with everything I've got until suddenly the entire metallic frame around me start to tremble and shake with an impeding orgasm.

"Oh my dark lord of the night!" The bus begins to stammer as the fire roars next to us. "Oh my dark lord of the night! Oh my dark lord of the fucking night!"

Each time Vlad repeats the phrase it grows a little louder until suddenly he's howling it at the top of his lungs. Seconds later, the bus is erupting within my asshole, his jizz blasting hard into me in a series of pulsing ejections. I push back against his length and hold, Vlad's dick fully inserted within as it continues to twitch and spasm. There is so much milky sperm that, seconds later, it comes spilling out from the tightly packed edges of my asshole and runs down my muscular legs in thick, pearly streaks.

"Oh fuck." I groan as I finally pull back, allowing Vlad's rod to slip out of me, followed by a tidal wave of spunk from my asshole. The mess of cum splatters down onto the bus floor below me.

"Now it's your turn." The vampire says. "Feed me."

I step out of the vehicle and walk around to the front as the fireplace continues to rage next to us.

"You want this cock?" I demand to know.

"Feed me!" The bus repeats.

"You much really want this fucking load, huh?" I continue, egging him on.

"Feed me!" Booms Vlad, his tone growing more and more impatient.

"What if I want you to beg me for it?" I ask.

Suddenly, the large velvet chair from across the room comes flying towards me, hitting me at the back of the knees and knocking me off of my feet. I land in the sitting position on its soft cushion. I'm carried forward towards the bus until I'm pressed right up against his massive, face, telekinetically held in place.

The vampire vehicle opens his mouth and takes me inside, swallowing graciously as he immediately gets to work with a series of slow, deliberate pumps. I throw my head back and close my eyes, savoring every moment of the vampire's wet lips as they travel up and down my length, wrapped tightly and expertly. With every pulse the bus grows faster, working me with an expert precision unlike anything I could ever have imagined.

His blowjob skills are more than any human could provide.

Soon enough. my entire body is quaking with ecstasy, the orgasmic sensations flooding through me in wave after looming wave. I clench my teeth, preparing for the intense sensation to hit and when it finally does I hiss loudly, my entire being overwhelmed by pleasure.

"I'm cumming!" I finally yell, my eyes rolling back into my head.

I can feel my load shoot hard into Vlad's waiting mouth and he swallows it immediately, sucking me down hungrily and then continuing to coax more of the seed out of me. Pumps of jizz erupt into the vampire's throat until, finally, I find myself completely dry and I fall back into the velvet chair, the bus throwing himself into reverse and pulling away slowly.

"That was fucking incredible." I tell the vampire. "Thank you."

Vlad smiles. "The pleasure was all mine."

"Really though," I continue, laying it on thick. "I didn't know what to expect when I first came up here to this castle, but I'm glad I trusted you. This was one of the best nights of my life." I suddenly crack a wry smile. "Thanks for not turning me into a bat."

Vlad grins back at me, his fangs glinting in the faint moonlight that streams through the windows above us. "Of course I wouldn't turn you into a bat."

Suddenly, I start to feel a strange sensation wash over me, my body aching from head to toe in a strange and unfamiliar way. I look down at my hands and see that they are changing color, becoming gray and tough.

"What the fuck!" I shout, trying to stand but immediately falling to the floor.

Vlad is cackling manically. "I won't turn you into a bat, but I never said anything about turning you into a bus!"

I can feel my body morphing and changing, elongating itself rapidly into the shape of a public transportation vehicle. "No!" I cry out, the sound of my voice transforming into a wild honk that echoes off of the castle walls.

3 ANGRY MAN POUNDED BY THE FEAR OF HIS LATENT GAYNESS OVER A DINOSAUR TRANSITIONING INTO A UNICORN

"What in the hell is this?" I ask aloud, the words simply falling out of my mouth as a photo fills my screen. I'm on some liberal news website that I normally wouldn't be caught dead on, but a friend of a friend emailed me the link.

I try desperately to make sense on what I'm seeing, because all that I can gather from this photo is a sexy, majestic unicorn looks ready to party. It's clearly a picture from some Hollywood photo shoot, which normally wouldn't rev me up on principal alone, but even *I* have to admit that this horned beast is absolutely gorgeous.

After ogling the unicorn for a bit, I click back to the email and make sure I've followed the correct link, reading the message aloud. "You won't believe what Bort Jenkins looks like now." The message reads. "This is so wrong."

I shake my head. Clearly, the friend who sent me this made a big mistake because the photo in question is definitely not of Bort Jenkins, tyrannosaurus athlete and star of the hit reality TV show, Borting Up With The Dinosaurs.

Instead, my buddy sent me the link to a sweet and sassy unicorn princess, and I can't say that I'm disappointed.

"God damn, you're a fine looking little piece of ass aren't you?" I groan, leaning back into my chair and unzipping my pants, excited to beat one out before the old battle axe gets home. Unfortunately, I get no more than two strokes in before that's exactly what happens.

"Carl!" My wife screams from outside the apartment, her shrill voice sending a sharp chill down my spine.

I immediately zip up my pants and jump to my feet, closing down the computer and walking over to the front door. I pull it open.

"Why the fuck is the door locked?" My wife screeches, pushing past me and almost knocking me over with her incredible size. She's holding a grocery bag in each hand, each of them seemingly overflowing with beer.

My wife sets the bags down on the kitchen table and then pulls out a tabloid magazine from one of the bags. "Did you see this?" She asks, thrusting the magazine into my face.

"Bambam." I say, trying to calm her down. "Chill."

"You expect me to chill when this kind of sinful behavior is being peddled to our kids?" Bambam screams.

"We don't have kids." I tell her, calmly.

"But if we did." My wife protests. "This is the kind of freak show the media would be rolling out for them."

I finally take the magazine from my wife's hands and look at the photo on the front, freezing abruptly as the image hits my eyes. It's the same painfully sexy unicorn that I had been beating off to just moments before.

"What is this?" I ask, suddenly very concerned.

"Bort Jenkins." Bambam tells me.

I stare at the magazine cover for a while and then look back into my wife's eyes, trying to figure out if she's joking or not.

"From that reality show?" I ask. "I don't think so."

"Honey." My wife says, taking the magazine out of my hands and holding it up to my face once more so I can get a really good look. She puts one of her chubby, long nailed fingers on the cover and taps it repeatedly. "This is Bort Jenkins now."

I can't help but laugh. "Bort Jenkins is a dinosaur, though."

"Not anymore." Bambam tells me.

There's something about the look in my wife's eyes that finally convinces me she's no longer joking, and as I glance back at the magazine one final time my blood runs cold. All of the pieces of the puzzle suddenly begin falling into place, swirling through my brain like a vicious tornado until eventually there is just nowhere else to run.

"He had a unichange." Bambam says, disgusted. "He's a unicorn now."

The words hit me like a punch in the gut, causing me to almost double over completely with their devastating force. I feel sick to my stomach as visions of the last ten minutes wash over me in brutal waves, particularly the part where I was pleasuring myself to the images of who I know is Bort. At first I try to desperately convince myself that I had never seen him as an attractive mystical creature, somehow knowing deep down inside that a vicious T-Rex lurked within. Despite my best efforts, though, I just can't do it. I know the truth of my actions.

"Sickening, right?" My wife says, not quite understanding the blank look on my face as my skin goes pale.

I nod. "Just terrible."

I stumble a little, almost losing my footing and then catching myself. "I think I need to get some fresh air." I blurt, staggering towards the door of our apartment.

"You don't want any dinner?" My wife asks.

"Maybe in a bit, I just…" I stammer, not knowing exactly what to say. I throw open the door and step outside, looking back at Bambam. "I just need a little time to myself, that's all."

I close the door behind me and, almost immediately, my wife starts screaming like a vicious dog whose been tied up too tight. Her words are almost incoherent, a stream of belligerence that I can't even begin to decipher. I stumble away quickly down the front walk, trying to put as much distance between me and her as possible, should she come stumbling out after me.

Soon, I'm walking down the side of the road, my legs carrying me wherever they want to go as my mind travels to all of its darkest corners imaginable. There's no denying it now, I was attracted to a unicorn that started as a dinosaur.

The admission fills me with so much dread and rage that I actually have to stop for a moment and find my way over into a nearby ditch, vomiting profusely as the cars continue to stream by. Someone honks loudly as they pass, probably mistaking me for a drunk, and I angrily flip them off as they disappear into the distance.

How could this have happened to me? A red blooded American male, I've loved unicorn's since the day I was born; their long, flowing manes, their sturdy, powerful hooves, and last but not least their shiny ivory horns that twist up towards the sun in a perfect spiral of beauty.

In fact, just thinking about them right now turns me on enough to develop a hearty, half-chubbed erection.

But Bort Jenkins was no unicorn, he was an abomination. I'm straight as an arrow, never once finding a dinosaur to be sexually attractive in any way. Sure, some of the football playing raptors on TV had impressive bodies, but if I'm looking to get myself off I'd much rather tune into the Unicorn Football League.

I suddenly shudder just thinking about the UFL, remember that they had recently allowed their first human player. What is this world coming to?

I fall to my knees on the side of the road and look up towards the sky, praying that god is looking down on me and listening. "What is wrong with me?" I cry out, my body filled with excruciating pain and overwhelming depression. "I'm not dinosexual! I'm not dinosexual!"

Not knowing what else to do, I let my head fall into my hands and begin to cry, the tears pouring down my face as a realize that I've become my own worst nightmare. I think back with pride to all the time's that I had bullied dinosexuals as a child, or posted hateful comments about them online. I used to be so cool, and now I'm just as bad as they are.

After kneeling here for some time I finally lift my head up, my gaze stopping on a bright neon sign that flickers just across the road from me in golden yellow. It's the local unicorn strip club, and never have I been more thankful for it's presence.

I climb to my feet and immediately head across the parking lot towards the blacked out front doors, ready to prove that I'm a real man who wants to bone hot unicorns, and only hot unicorns.

I practically kick open the doors as I reach them, flashing the bouncer my ID and then immediately taking a seat at the very front of the stage.

"Alright!" Slams a booming voice over the club's loudspeaker. "Our next dancer comes to you all the way from Tennessee. He's a rootin' tootin' cowboy named Dasher and he's ready to clop his way into your heart. Everyone give it up for the one… the only… Dasher Sprinkles!"

Seconds later the most incredible, muscular unicorn I have ever seen steps out into the stage, dressed up to the nines in a very slutty little cowboy outfit that he immediately get's to work stripping out of. The whole world around me seems to stop as Dasher work's his magic, clopping back and forth and then eventually taking a few spins around the pole.

Several other men quickly join me at the front of the stage and soon enough the money is raining down onto the gorgeous young dancer. Dasher is loving every second of it, putting on a show like nothing I've ever seen.

Yet somehow, I'm not getting hard.

I look down towards my cock, which rests just behind a thin layer of fabric within my pants. "Come on." I coax. "You love this shit, bro."

My dick doesn't move a muscle, absolutely refusing to affirm my strong attraction to the handsome unicorn.

"Come on." I coax, beads of sweat forming on my forehead as the anxiety continues to blossom within me. "Come on."

I suddenly feel a twitch of something lustful in my groin but before it can get any further the song ends and Dasher begins to collect his money from the stage.

"Wait!" I shout frantically, suddenly right back where I started. "Don't go!"

Despite all of the chatter around us, Dasher hears me and looks up from his bouquet of dollar bills. "You want a private dance, baby?" The unicorn asks.

"Yes." I nod frantically. "Please."

The next thing I know, Dasher Sprinkles has taken my hand in his hoof and is leading me across the strip club to a curtained off back room. I follow him excitedly, my heart pounding hard within my chest.

"Why don't you just have a seat?" Dasher offers once we're all alone, leading me over to a red velvet couch and then closing the curtains behind us.

The unicorn immediately gets to work swaying his hips back and forth, his muscular body entrancing me more and more with every movement.

"God damn, you look so good." I say, unable to contain my excitement.

"Oh yeah?" The unicorn coos. "You really think so?"

"I know so." I tell him. "I'm not some dinosaur lover or anything like that. I know good unicorn tail when I see it."

The dancer freezes suddenly, stopping abruptly as my words hit his ears. "What did you say?" Dasher questions.

"Oh, I just meant that I'm not some dinochaser." I say. "I'm a man's man, you know?"

The look of the unicorns face changes slightly, his once joyful expression transforming to one of contempt and utter disappointment. "So *real men* don't like dinosaurs?" The unicorn asks.

"Well, yeah." I stammer, not exactly sure what I should say or why this dancer is getting so upset with me.

Suddenly, an perfect example dawns on me. "Like Bort Jenkins, right? He was born as a dinosaur, that's the way that god mad him and he should just stay that way! It's the natural order of things."

Dasher shakes his head. "You're disgusting. Get out."

"What?" I shout, standing up. "I'm giving you a fucking compliment here."

"You honestly think you have the right to tell Bort Jenkins, or any other dinosaur for that matter, what they're allowed to do with their own bodies?" The now furious unicorn dancer yells as bouncers start approaching from either side. "What fucking right do you have?"

The massive bouncers grab me by either arm and I immediately struggle against them, enraged by the way this plan is turning out.

"What are you asking?" I scream at the unicorn dancer as the bouncers pick me up and start carrying me towards the door. "Are you asking if I hate dinosaurs that become unicorns? Well the answer is yes! Yes I do!"

The entire strip club starts booing me, a few patrons actually helping to clear the way as the bouncers carry me out.

The next thing I know, the front door of the club opens and I'm being thrown through the air, hurtling several feet before slamming hard onto the pavement and rolling end over end. I tumble for a while and then eventually come to rest, bloody and bruised, while the club door slams shut behind me.

"Dinosaurs are dinosaurs! Unicorns are unicorns!" I scream out into the night. "Deal with it!"

It takes a few minutes but eventually I manage to drag myself to my feet and begin the defeated walk back home to the apartment. It's late now, and very few cars continue up and down the road. Instead of rumbling engines, my senses are overwhelmed by the chirping crickets who call out from somewhere deep inside the nearby forest.

"I should probably cut through." I think to myself, realizing now just how long I've been gone. My wife is going to kill me when I get home and, as much as I dread returning, the sooner I get there the better.

I immediately veer off of the road and into the word, muttering to myself under my breath as though anything I say could possibly change the fact that I had, just moments before, thought a dinosaur was attractive enough to jerk off to.

The trees grown thicker and thicker around me as I continue deeper still, and eventually the moon above is blocked out by the crisscross of gnarled branches that hang above.

"Carl." A voice suddenly moans. I stop and immediately turn around to look behind me.

There's nothing there.

"Hello?" I call out, my voice bouncing back to me across the assortment of twisting trees.

Eventually, I begin walking again, but it's not long before I hear the voice for a second time. I spin back around, once more greeted by absolutely nothing.

"You don't want to mess with me tonight!" I call out into the dark woods. "Don't fuck with me 'cause I ain't scared."

"Not scared?" I voice suddenly asks.

I spin and nearly fall over backwards in shock at what I see. There, hovering before me, is a massive, misty apparition in the shape of a face. It floats menacingly, it's form changing and shifting slightly in the wind but, for the most part, retaining the look of an enormous hollow skull with ghostly nude bodies flowing through it. I lean in closer to see that the muscular bodies within this thing's ethereal form belong to dinosaurs.

"What are you?" I ask, my voice trembling.

The skull laughs. "You already know the answer to that one, Carl, you just can't accept it yet?"

I shake my head. "I don't know what you're talking about."

"Do you know why you're so afraid of Bort Jenkins?" The skull asks me.

"I'm not afraid of Bort Jenkins." I counter. "I'm angry at the example he sets!"

"A lot of the time anger is just fear in disguise." The skull explains. "This is one of those times."

I shake my head, not wanting to accept the words that are being thrown my way. "Fuck that, I don't want to hear this." I say.

"I know, I know." Chuckles the hazy skull. "But I'm not going to go away anytime soon because I'm a part of you, Carl. You might as well just deal with your feelings right here and now."

"What feelings?" I scream at the appreciation, fed up.

"The fact that you're attracted to a unicorn who was once a dinosaur makes you question your own sexuality." Explains the skull. "And the only way for you to deal with that is to say that there's something wrong with the unicorn, when in fact the only person with a problem is you."

"No! No! No!" I shout, putting my hands over my ears as I fall to my knees. "You're lying! This is just a dinosaur trick!"

"Afraid not." Says the skull. "And while we're at it, I guess you should know that you're a repressed homosexual, too."

Suddenly, the skull has gone a little too far for any of this be believable. I crack a smile and stand back up. "You had me going there for a minute, but the gay thing is just a little too much."

"You we're just at a bar full of male strippers." The skull says flatly.

"Male unicorn strippers." I explain. "Big difference."

The skull shakes from side to side mid air. "There's no difference, Carl."

His words repeat over and over again within my head, bouncing around in an endless loop that seems to drift deeper and deeper into the most hidden parts of my soul. Eventually, I can't hear anything else. Tears begin to well up in my eyes, my emotions suddenly too overwhelming to contain within my body.

"Oh my god." I stammer, the entire universe suddenly opening up before me in a blast of cathartic realization. "I hate Bort Jenkins because I'm jealous of him. He's so open with his sexuality while I keep mine pushed deep down inside, hidden away."

The skull nods. "That's correct."

"I don't want to hide anymore." I say. "Like you said, there's no difference."

"It's all love." The skull agrees.

"I'm gay." I say, the words fulling my soul with beautiful warmth. "I like unicorns… and dinosaurs."

Suddenly, the misty skull is swirling around me, enveloping me in its sensual touch. I close my eyes and let out a soft moan, reeling from the sensation of being held by a personified version of my own repressed sexual identity.

"I want you." I say. "I want to be who I'm supposed to be."

The mist begins to take shape around me, forming personified manifestations of my latent gayness. I have to admit, they look good; hunky ethereal men with absolutely massive erections projecting out from their bodies.

I look down and suddenly realize that, I too, am hard. After all of this effort, nothing was more arousing than losing my own sexual inhibitions.

Finally, I just can't take it anymore, overwhelmed with ecstasy as I drop to my knees. I start to beat off the mist furiously, a cock and each hand as I make my way around the circle.

"Oh my god." I say, overwhelmed by the forest of dick that surrounds me. "I can't believe how gay I really am. All of this time spent hating people who a different than me and now I realize that I'm just as different as they are."

"In your own way." Says the mist. "We're all different in our own way, and that's okay."

The personified sexual fear seem to enjoy my touch, groaning in turn as I take my time with each one of their rods. They rock their hips to the movement of my hands, closing their eyes tightly as my firm grip pleasures them.

Suddenly, one of the ethereal forms puts his hands behind my head and pushes foreword, thrusting his massive shaft between my lips. I swallow him gladly, taking as much length as I can until he's pressing hard against my gag reflex. I try my best to relax and allow him past, but it's just too much to bear and suddenly I'm retching loudly, sputtering as I pull his rod out in a flurry of spit. I gasp for air, trying to collect myself as more and more hazy cocks are pressed against my mouth, anxious for their turn.

Seconds later, I'm taking the latent gayness deep once again, hungrily swallowing his massive dick and letting it expertly slip down into my depths. Somehow I manage to relax enough to allow him passage beyond my gag reflex, and the next thing I know his balls are pressed tightly against my chin, his cock completely disappearing within my neck. The strange being holds me there for a moment, enjoying the sensation of controlling me just as much as I enjoy being controlled. He starts to push me up and down slightly, using me as his own private play toy for a moment before letting me up in a frantic gasp for air.

The cocks continue to be thrust between my lips from every direction, and I quickly lose track of just how many I've taken. I spend a little time with each one, bobbing my head over there length as I use my hands to beat off the others two at a time. I lick up and down on their enormous shafts, running my tongue from balls to tip before swallowing them down again. The scene is frantic and wild, a completely depraved expression of all my pent up sexual bigotry that's been dying to be exorcised.

At this point my dick is absolutely aching to be touched, throbbing between my legs as I yearn to be penetrated up the ass by any one of their massive misty cocks.

"Please." I gasp, pulling a member from my throat and looking up at the supernatural beings with huge doe eyes. "I need to be fucked."

One of the ethereal begins quickly drops to his knees behind me and begins to align his dick with my tight, puckered asshole. I look back at him and give a playful wink, then cry out loudly as he thrusts forward and stretches my tightness around the girth of his huge rod. His size is incredible, filling me completely as he pushes in and out with a slow, powerful grace.

"Oh fuck." I moan, my hands tightly gripping the green grass in front of me. "That personified sexual redneck fear feels so fucking good inside this tight butthole!"

The latent gayness hammering me from behind soon finds a pleasant rhythm and speeds up, his thrusts becoming a powerful pulsing slam against my round ass. Meanwhile, the misty apparitions around my face have stepped back and formed an orderly line, the first one shoving his cock down my throat so that I'm now being pounded from both ends. They push in and out of me in tandem with one another, timing their movements so that they're slamming my muscular body back and forth across their lengths like I'm some beautiful human sex-kabob.

One things for sure, though, they know what they're doing, and it's not long before I find myself trembling as a prostate orgasm begins to blossom within me. I reach down and try to help it along, using my hand to rapidly stroke my throbbing cock as the quakes of pleasure continue to course through my body. I moan into the dick that fills my mouth, preparing for a powerful climax but then suddenly the cocks within me pull out and another two take their place, instantly starting the process over again.

These new misty men are just as hung as the first, and they waste no time picking up speed as they plow my tight holes. I brace myself against their thrusts, my eyes rolling back into my head as I struggle to handle the intense waves of pleasure being pounded through my body. They continue like this for a good while and then, like before, switch out with another pair of ethereal beings.

Eventually, all of the manifestations have had a turn within me. I'm still aching to cum but the mist men still have much more in store for my once closeted body.

One of the creatures lies down onto the ground next to me and instructs me to climb onto him, which I do happily. I straddle his body with my manly legs, and from where I sit I can now fully appreciate his ridiculously muscular yet foggy chest, which heaves and expands with every deep breath. I run my hands down the washboard abs of my own latent gayness and then take his rock hard dick in my hand, maneuvering it to the entrance of my tightness and then slipping down onto him as I impale my reamed asshole onto his rod. I slide down his length slowly, letting out a soft whimper when I reach the hilt and then start in with a slow grind.

"I was wrong about everything." I confess, my body tingling with absolute ecstasy. My swoops against the personified fear grow harder and harder, rapidly gaining speed until I am hammering down onto him with all of my force. My latent gayness helps me along with his powerful arms, taking my hips in his hands and guiding me into perfect alignment with his massive, swollen cock.

At this point I'm completely overwhelmed, my brain flooding with the most depraved, gay sexual thoughts possible. I crave more pleasure, more sex, more cock.

"Someone get over here and shove another dick up my fucking ass!" I suddenly demand, surprising even myself. "I need to be double fucked right now!"

One of the misty beings quickly takes his position behind me, squatting down and aligning his massive cock with the puckered rim of my already filled asshole. It's a tense fit, the muscle of my ass fighting against his advances as he slowly pushes the head of his dick into my anal seal.

"Harder!" I command, looking back over my shoulder with a wicked fire in my eyes. "Just shove that fat dick inside of me! Punish me for being such a bad, bad little bigot!"

The latent gayness takes my words to heart and immediately thrusts foreword, hard, driving his dick up into my rectum in one powerful thrust. I scream aloud in a mixture of pain and pleasure, my entire body in shock from the bizarre sensation of two giant cocks fucking me in the same asshole.

The next thing I know, the mists are pumping back and forth within me, pulsing together so that their shafts create an incredible rhythm of pleasure. It's unlike anything I've ever experienced.

"Fuck me! Fuck me!" I'm screaming in a belligerent trance until suddenly one of the hazy men steps foreword and shoves his cock down my throat, cutting me off and turning my shrieks into a strange muted gargle.

Eventually, the ethereal creatures pull out and flip me over so that my back rests firmly against the latent sexual repression beneath me, while a second one pummels my ass from the front. Of course, a third misty man takes my mouth and suddenly I'm back where I started, with every gay hole filled to the max.

The mist begins to trade places within me, fucking me hard with their massive rods and then, right when I'm just about ready to cum, they pull out and let another one of the strange beings take their place. I quickly find myself lost in the frenzy of dick, my mind melting into a sexed up, cock hungry animal just aching to climax.

No sooner have I lost myself in their tornado of dick, when suddenly that familiar orgasmic sensation starts to bloom within me again, coming on strong and fast. I reach down between my legs and attack my cock, rapidly stroking myself as the sensations within me grow bigger and bigger, and then suddenly they erupt within my body. I let out a powerful scream that reverberates through the dick in my mouth, my eyes closed tight and my stomach clenched tighter. Wave after wave of ecstasy pulses through me and for a brief moment I forget where I am, leaving my shell in an out-of-body experience. Jizz erupts from my cock, splattering everywhere.

I finish cumming and then immediately collapse onto the ground next to the misty begins, who stand up and form a tight circle around me while they beat their dicks furiously. I look up at them through a lustful haze and beg for their jizz.

"Cover me with your fucking gay loads." I command. "I need your seed all over this bigoted bro face."

It's not long before the strange creatures are beginning to blow, the first two of them shooting their loads onto my face in crossed ropes of milky white semen. It splatters across me and runs down my cheeks, a few white droplets catching playfully in my eyelashes. I open my mouth and stick out my tongue, then catch the next load as it sails through the air towards me.

"More!" I demand. "I need more gay cum!"

Load after load rains down onto me, covering my entire face with a pearly glaze of jizz. I lick it off my lips happily, swallowing hard and then finally taking the last one of them right on the forehead.

The mist fall back and find seats around the room, panting with exhaustion.

"Holy fuck." I say aloud, reaching up and touching the thick layer of spunk that's plastered onto my face.

I step through the door of the apartment and find my wife, Bambam, waiting silently on the couch, her teeth gritted in anger.

"Where the fuck were you?" Bambam asks.

"I had to think about some things." I tell her.

"I bet." My wife retorts. "It's another woman isn't it?"

"Actually." I tell her. "It's another man."

Bambam starts to laugh. "What the fuck are you talking about?"

"It's another man." I repeat. "Myself."

My wife stops laughing.

"You can get the fuck out." I say.

Bambam's face goes through a quick series of emotions, from confusion, to utter rage, and then to amusement. "You don't have what it takes to kick me out of your life." She snarls. "I know courage and you don't have it. I'm more of a man than you'll ever be."

"Get out." I repeat.

Bambam stands up and walks over to the door, at which point a grab the tabloid magazine off of the kitchen table and push it into her hands, Bort Jenkin's smiling Unicorn face still there on the cover.

"You want to learn something about courage." I say. "Read this."

I slam the door, and begin my brand new life.

4 MY ASS IS HAUNTED BY THE GAY UNICORN COLONEL

As I approach the old plantation house, my body fills with a strange sensation. It's a feeling that is not entirely new to me, but it is also one strictly reserved for occasions of extreme tension and caution. To call this emotion fear is flat-out incorrect, it is not fear but something even deeper and more subliminal. This feeling is the remnant of a long forgotten instinct, one that taps deep into my mind and then connects itself to some other world, some other plane of existence.

And then, just like that, the feeling disappears.

A chill runs down my spine as I look up at the windows of the old mansion, framed perfectly between two large weeping willows here in the deep forest of northern Georgia.

For a moment, I catch a glimpse of someone standing in the window of a second story bedroom, a unicorn with a long white mane and a large, pearly white horn. The majestic beast moves out of the way as soon as I see him, letting the curtain fall back into place.

"Hello there!" The voice on an elderly woman suddenly calls from the front porch. "Welcome to Blue Bayou Bed and Breakfast!"

I smile and wave as my gaze falls upon a small old lady in her casual summer wear, hurrying down the steps to greet me. When I booked my room I had no idea I would be receiving such a warm welcome, and it's a pleasant relief from the usual indifference that I get from places like this.

Get in, pay us, get out, is usually the motto, especially when the ghost sightings have reached a level of notoriety that turns an establishment into less of a bed and breakfast, and more of a tourist trap.

"You must be Roger." The old woman says, taking one of my bags. "I'm Melody. It's nice to meet you, come along right this way."

It all happens to fast that I barely have time to protest. "Oh come on now, I'll carry my bags up!" I tell her, legitimately worried that she's about to break a bone simply hoisting up my leather weekender.

"Don't be silly!" Melody creaks in her own cheerful way. "You're my guest, I so rarely get guests anymore."

I sigh and follow her up the front porch and into the house. "I thought people were coming from all over the world to catch a glimpse of Colonel Peach's ghost, shouldn't that be bringing in some business?"

"Oh, it did for a while." Melody tells me, placing my bag in the entryway and then leading me into the dining room. "But it seems like people aren't interested in history like they used to be. Nobody cares about an old civil war spirit I guess"

As I round the corner of the dining room I'm immediately hit with the pleasant aroma of savory, delicious food. There are two places set at the end of the table, one for Melody and one for me, and an entire assortment of roast vegetables, grilled meats, and a cauldron of soup in the middle.

"Oh my god." I gasp in astonishment. "You can't be serious, this looks incredible."

"Well, I figured you probably had a long journey today so I figured I'd whip up some dinner." Melody explains. "It's just the two of us tonight but I reckoned that if I'm gonna go through the trouble of cooking, I might as well do it right."

Melody sits down in her chair and I follow suit, smiling graciously as she dishes up some of the creamy soup into a bowl and hands it to me. Even if I don't see any colonial ghosts on this trip, this is still one hell of a bed and breakfast.

"Can I ask?" I start. "If it's just the two of us here, then who was that unicorn upstairs when I drove in?"

"Upstairs?" Melody asks, slightly confused.

"Yeah, he was staring down at me from the far left window." I explain.

Melody freezes as she hears this, a smile slowly creeping across her wrinkled old face. "A unicorn, you say?"

I nod, not quite seeing what the big deal is at this point.

Melody sits in silence for just a moment longer and then stands up. "Dinner can wait for just a moment, I think you'll want to see this." The elderly woman leaves the dining room and heads back across the hall to what appears to be the main living quarters; two sofas, a fireplace, a mantle, and hanging above it a massive oil painting.

I follow Melody, but the second that I lay my eyes upon the strange portrait I stop, gazing up in wonder at the incredible sight that suspends before more. There in the thick strokes of vivid color sits a familiar face, one that I recognize almost immediately. It's the unicorn that I spotted in the window upstairs.

The creature looks absolutely regal, sitting atop a horse with the wind blowing through his sparkling unicorn mane. He's wearing a dark uniform and carrying a flag that waves in the wind behind him.

"Is that the unicorn that you saw in the window?" Melody asks.

I nod.

"That's Colonel Peach, he's been dead since the civil war." The old woman informs me.

This information is almost too shocking to comprehend, a revelation so strange that I have to silently repeat it back to myself over and over again until finally it clicks. I had just seen the ghost with my very own eyes.

Melody is kind enough to let me stay in the Colonel's old chambers tonight, which is precisely the room that I saw his single-horned ghost just hours earlier. The room is slightly chilly but beautifully arranged, featuring heavy oak furniture that has probably been here since the manor was built all those years ago.

The room itself gives me that same spooky feeling that I got upon arrival at these haunted grounds, an eerie kind of presence that seems to be lurking within each and every shadow.

As it grows later, the silver moonlight begins to stretch longer into the room. I'm lying in bed, reading quietly over some recently published papers on the paranormal.

Suddenly, I jump, a loud knock against the hardwood floors drawing my attention to the closed bedroom door before me.

"Hello?" I call out. "Miss Melody?"

This particular room has not yet been retrofitted for modern electricity, so I have been reading by candlelight. I glance over as the tiny flame flickers and struggles to stay alive, fighting against some strange cold wind as it gusts through the room with supernatural speed.

There is no response to my inquisitive call, but as I listen closely I can faintly hear what appears to be the wild cries of a civil war battle, the sounds echoing within my ears. I can hear the clap of muskets firing and the shouting of battle commands. A bungle rings out over the sound of thundering hooves as soldiers ride into battle. It's an utterly frightening illusion in its stark realness, and can only be perceived as false because it simply makes no sense.

My heart pounding within my chest, I watch as the doorknob to my bedroom begins to turn slowly. There is a loud metallic click and then moments later the door itself starts to open as a dark figure emerges.

"You called?" Comes the voice of Melody.

I let out a massive sigh of both relief and, of course, disappointment. I'm here to see a ghost, after all.

"Did you…" I stammer. "Did you hear that?"

"Hear what?" Melody asks.

"All of that fighting? Those war sounds?" I continue.

Melody just shakes her head. "No, I'm afraid that I didn't, but it sounds like being in this room has spooked you quite a bit. Are you sure you don't want me to put you up somewhere else?"

"Oh no." I tell the caring elderly woman. "I'm here to see the colonel, and this seems like the best place to do it."

Melody turns to leave and then stops for a moment, hesitating. She turns back around. "Roger, why is it that you are so interested in seeing these spirits for yourself."

I take a deep breath, closing my book and setting it down on the bedside table next to me. "Long ago, when I was just a nineteen-year-old fresh out of school, I took a trip to Spain. It was incredible, the food, the men." I tell her, letting Melody in on a subtle hint about my sexuality, in case she didn't already notice. "Anyway, I was there for a month and during that time I met a beautiful white unicorn named Paulo. He was so handsome, and so good to me. I rode around the city on his back all day and, in the evenings, Paulo would take me back to his flat and we would make love."

Melody gets a faint little twinkle in her eye. "Awe, that sounds very sweet."

I nod. "It was, it was. Back in those days unicorn and human relationships were looked down upon, but we didn't care. When Paulo and me were together it was like we could take on anything, change the world. I don't know if you believe in soul mates, Miss Melody, but I can assure you they are real."

"I believe." Melody says, smiling to herself.

"Then I'm guessing you know what it's like to loose your soul mate as well." I say, tearing up a bit. "You see, Paulo the unicorn was hoof hearted, meaning his heart was the size of a hoof, much too small for a unicorn of his size. I didn't know at the time, but he only had a few weeks left to live."

As I say this Melody places her hand over her heart, hurting for me as I remember my long lost lover.

"After, Paulo passed away." I continue. "I've been obsessed with the afterlife. I just want to know if he's still out there somewhere, my handsome Spanish unicorn."

"I'm sure he's out there." Melody assures me. "Looking down on you."

We stand in silence for a moment, before Melody nods and backs out into the hallway. She closes the door quietly behind her.

I grab my book off of the bedside table and start to read again.

I only make it a few sentences in before the words start to blur together in a meaningless mess. Getting emotional about Paulo my unicorn lover has made me tired, and before I know it I find myself drifting off to sleep.

I'm not sure how long I've been out when I awaken, but I sit up abruptly and suck in a huge gasp of air. My book, which had been resting on my lap, falls to the floor next to the bed with a light thump as I attempt to figure out exactly what it was that startled me awake so abruptly.

Faintly, I can hear my own name drifting through the night air. It sounds as though it's coming from right outside my window, emanating from somewhere in the front yard of this spooky old manor.

Cautiously, I climb to my feet and tiptoe over to the window, looking out onto the moon soaked lawn.

My breath catches in my throat. There before me, in all of his majestic unicorn ghost glory, is Colonel Peach. The unicorn colonel sits atop his powerful steed in full uniform, looking up at me as I gaze down at him. He's just as handsome as the painting that hangs downstairs, and despite my best efforts I almost immediately find myself just as aroused as I am afraid.

The sound of my own name still echoes through the trees. "Roger, roger." It's as if the unicorn colonel is begging me to run down to him and let him pick me up in his big, strong, ghost arms.

Compelled by some supernatural force, I turn away from the window, ready to sprint down to the colonel and give myself to him, but he's already here with me. I stop abruptly, shocked as I discover that the ghost has somehow instantly appeared within my room, no more than five feet away.

Now that I'm this close I can see that the colonel's body is slightly transparent, shimmering faintly as it sparkles with a strange unicorn magic. I can also see now how incredibly handsome this beast is, from his pearly horn to his heavy hooves, which poke out from the pants of his beautiful civil war uniform.

"Roger." The unicorn colonel says. "I have come here to deliver a message from beyond. I have come to bring you a message from Paulo."

The sound of my dead lovers name causes my heart to skip a beat. "What is it?" I stammer. "Tell me."

As I say the words I can feel a slight tingling begin deep within my ass, in a place that only Paulo could reach with his massive unicorn cock. In this moment I realize that Paulo's spirit is inside of me, haunting my ass.

"Paulo has a message from the great beyond." The unicorn colonel tells me. "A message of passion and fire, a message of love."

"I can feel it." I admit. "I can feel him deep within my butt."

The unicorn colonel nods. "Yes, but he's always been there, haunting your ass while you worked, slept… cried."

"He was there all along." I repeat.

The unicorn colonel nods. "Even though he's not powerful enough yet to manifest himself in physical form, he wanted me to pleasure you the way that he cannot."

At first I'm not exactly sure what Colonel Peach is saying, the strange invitation bouncing off of my brain a few times before finally sinking in. When I realize what he's getting at, however, I can't help being overwhelmed with a powerful arousal that immediately floods into my veins.

"You mean, Paulo want's us to fuck?" I ask, my voice trembling.

"He want's to give you pleasure." Says the Colonel Peach. "And right now this is the best way for him to do that."

I close my eyes and try to grapple with the idea of giving myself to a lover other than Paulo. Since Paulo's death, I hadn't slept with a single soul, unicorn or otherwise, and the idea alone seemed daunting. Still, just the suggestion had gotten my so worked up, my dick rock hard within my boxer briefs and just begging to be unleashed. Besides, this is what Paulo wants for me.

I swallow hard and then step forward so that I'm just inches away from the ghostly unicorn. "I want you." I say, letting my hand drift lower and lower until it reaches Colonel Peach's belt buckle, which I unclasp.

"I want you, too." The handsome dead unicorn says, finally giving in.

I undo his belt and then slowly unzip the Colonel's pants, which reveal no civil war era underwear underneath.

Instead, I'm greeted by this sight of his beautiful throbbing member, which springs forth from the fabric as soon as I let it. Colonel Peach is hard as a rock and aching to be touched, his enormous unicorn cock jutting fiercely out towards me.

I smile and slowly drop down into a squat before the beast, so that his shaft is pointed directly at my chiseled face, and then look up at him with my soulful gay eyes.

"Do you want me to suck you off?" I ask playfully. "For Paulo?"

The unicorn colonel doesn't answer, silent for a moment as he takes me in with his eerie, ghostly presence. He seems just as fascinated by me as I am of him.

"I said, do you want me to suck off that big, fat, unicorn cock of yours?" I repeat.

Finally, Colonel Peach breaks his silence; the single word barely making it out of his gently parted lips alive. "Yes."

With that, I open wide and engulf Colonel Peach's cock with my mouth, pushing my head down along the length of his shaft until I reach the edge of my gag reflex. I close my eyes and focus, relaxing my body until finally I feel comfortable going even deeper. Eventually, I reach the base of his shaft with my lips, my face pushed right up against Colonel Peach's hard unicorn abs as he fills my throat entirely.

The creature lets out a long, satisfied moan, his entire body shaking from my masterful deep throat. I can feel the colonel's hoof hands press gently on the back of my head and hold me there, hesitating, as if he's still not entirely sure that he wants to commit to this favor for a ghostly friend.

But the ship has already sailed, and as I reach up and begin to play with the beast's hanging balls that rest against my chin, the feeling is just too much for Colonel Peach to ignore. He starts to pump me up and down his shaft, slowly at first and then gaining speed as the waves of pleasure start to overwhelm him.

I look up at the colonel and we lock eyes, his cock planted firmly in my throat. I can't help but give him a playful little wink, and suddenly he's over the edge completely, a crazed look of sexual passion overwhelming his expression as he rocks his hips against me.

I slowly pull his unicorn pants father and farther down until he's able to step out of them. Releasing Colonel Peach from my mouth I stand up and give him a deep kiss.

"Lie down on the bed." I instruct.

The unicorn ghost starts to protest slightly but I'm firm with my instructions. I grab his hoof in my hand and then force it down the front of my boxer brief's, letting him feel the hard thickness of my massive rod.

"Do you want this dick?" I ask plainly.

"I can't." The colonel explains. "I'm a unicorn, I'll break it."

"Me and Paulo used to fuck on our bed all the time." I tell him. "So that's what we're gonna do."

The unicorn understands, and moments later he removes his uniform completely and climbs up into the massive oak bed, which creaks under the weight of his massive unicorn body.

"You look good." I coo, egging the beast on.

Finding his confidence, Colonel Peach sprawled out on his bed before me, his cock hard and standing at full attention. It's much longer and thicker than I had even realized when it was engulfed within my mouth, and now that I can fully inspect the translucent, ghostly shaft's incredible size I'm even more impressed.

I slowly strut across the hardwood floors towards Colonel Peach, enjoying the way that his eyes flicker and dance across my ripped, muscular body. At this point, he can't help but stare.

Seductively, I climb up onto the bed and crawl towards him, popping my gay ass out into the air as I go and then eventually positioning myself directly over his huge body. I take Colonel Peach's hooves and pull them above his head, controlling him completely as I make my way down his ripped chest and abs with a series of sensual kisses.

Despite my newfound confidence, however, I find myself trembling with anticipation and fear. I know that it's Paulo who want's this, but I can't keep myself from imaging my lover watching over us, analyzing every move that we make. Moments later, however, I feel that familiar tingle deep within my ass; a reminder.

I close my eyes and take a deep breath, and then let go of any reservations I had left within me. Immediately, I reach down and take Colonel Peach's huge rod into my hand, aligning him with the puckered tightness of my gay asshole.

"Oh fuck." The colonel groans instinctively as I push down onto him, letting out a soft moan of my own as the powerful beast slides up inside of me, my asshole expanding to it's limits in an effort to take his brutal insertion.

His presence fills me with a sensation that is familiar and warm, a distant memory that had been locked away until this very moment. I bite my lip instinctively and start to grind against him with firm, deep swoops of my hips.

I'm not fully prepared for the long forgotten sensation of being entered by a unicorn lover, and almost immediately I'm beside myself with pleasure, my body trembling and quaking as I ride him. It's as if all the sexual bliss that I've been staving myself from has been here the whole time, hiding away in some dark corner of my being and just waiting to be released by the right gay beast.

"Oh my god." I pant loudly, repeating the words over and over again. "Oh my god, oh my god."

Colonel Peach's hooves are on my hips, helping to pull me up and down across him in an incredible pulsing rhythm. I can feel all of his powerful strength though this minor touch; he's showing restraint, his body handling me firmly but with care.

"Let go." I tell him. "Just pound me like my dead unicorn lover would."

That does the trick. Suddenly, Colonel Peach is sitting up and flipping me over with his muscular unicorn legs, turning me around to that I'm facing away from him on my hands and knees. I look back at him and smile.

There's a loud crack as Colonel Peach slaps my ass with a hoof, hard, then he grabs me by my hips and pulls me back towards him with ease. He takes his cock and maneuvers it into the entrance of my anal tightness. There's a fire in Colonel Peach's eyes as he thrusts into me, the massive rod filling my butthole entirely as I cry out with a yelp of pleasure. Colonel Peach wastes no time now, immediately getting to work as he rams my body from behind.

I grip tightly onto the bed sheets in front of me, bracing myself against the unicorn colonel's powerful slams. There is an animalistic nature to his thrusting now, more brazen than sensual, but the ghostly creature still knows exactly how to hit my prostate on the inside. Somehow, this is even more of a turn on than before, his gentlemanly demeanor finally cracking before my very eyes, the poker face slipping away and finally revealing the sexual beast underneath.

"Harder!" I scream back at him, never more turned on my entire life. "Fuck me harder like the little human twink that I am!"

Colonel Peach doesn't need to be told twice, picking up speed until he is absolutely pummeling me with everything that he's got, slamming my asshole from behind with gay reckless abandon.

I reach down and grab a hold of my cock, beating myself off furiously.

Deep within my stomach I can now feel the first beautiful sparks of orgasm begin to fly, lighting a tiny fire that slowly but surely begins to creep its way out across my body. I can't help but start to tremble and quake as the sensation consumes me, filling me with a strange warmth from head to toe.

The tremors of pleasant sensation keep coming in awesome waves, the space between them drawing shorter until finally it just becomes one giant ball of pleasure that envelops my body. I clench my teeth tightly and let out a long hiss, frantically grasping at the last straws of reality before a powerful orgasm pushes me over the edge.

I'm outside myself now, looking down at my body as I cum harder than I ever have. Jizz erupts from the head of my cock, splattering onto the bed sheets before me in a beautiful pattern of milky white. It's a satisfaction that can barely be described, a blinding fullness that consumes me perfectly. I throw my head back and let out a howl of ecstasy, unable to contain all of this sensation within. In this moment, I know that Paulo is with me, haunting my ass with Colonel Peach.

I don't have long to mull on this, however, because seconds later the colonel is shaking as well, his massive unicorn body preparing for an orgasm of his own.

"Cum all over me!" I demand fiercely. "Shoot that load all over this handsome gay face of mine!"

Colonel Peach pulls out and gives his cock three final pumps with his hand, then grips tightly against the base as a rope of hot jizz ejects out across me. It feels nice against my skin; playful almost.

The ghostly unicorn throws his head back and neighs, his abs held firm as several more pumps of cum eject from his shaft and splatter across my chin.

"Thank you." I tell him when the spunk finally stops falling.

The unicorn looks down at me with a look of satisfaction plastered across his face, then moments later evaporates into nothing.

"I hope you found what you were looking for." Melody tells me as I carry my bags out to the car.

I smile. "I did, actually."

The old woman is very pleased with this answer and, despite only knowing me for a day, gives me one final hug. "You're a very nice young man." She informs me.

"Thanks, Melody." I tell her.

"I hope that one day our paths will cross again." The old woman says as she releases her grip and I climb into the driver's seat of my car.

I look up at her. "Are you kidding me?" I'll be back within the week."

"Really?" Melody asks, her eyes lighting up.

"Just don't forget to put some more of that amazing soup on!"

As I drive away from the old manor I catch a glimpse of two ghostly unicorns standing off at the edge of a nearby field, patiently awaiting my return.

5 THE STATE OF CALIFORNIA STALKS MY BUTTHOLE

As I see him climb out of the pool, abs rippling while the water cascades down off of his incredible body, I try my hardest to look away and avert my bumbling stare.

"Is it him?" my friend Jonah asks me, glancing over the top of his sunglasses.

"I don't know," I reply, honestly not quite sure.

The thing is, it looks exactly like him; tall with tan skin and broad shoulders, a little crooked to the right and a vast empire of agriculture throughout the middle. But if this is the case, and we actually are staring at the shirtless form of the hot and sexy state of California, then why is he here on the East Coast?

"Go talk to him," Jonah urges me, elbowing me in the side as we watch from the pool bar.

"I don't think it's him," I say. "What would be doing all the way over here in Miami?"

Jonah shrugs. "Taking a vacation? I don't see why not, everybody has to get out of town sometime."

"Yeah, but not everyone has Hollywood to run," I tell him.

"Oh my god, don't look. Here he comes." Jonah says suddenly, trying to get me to avert my eyes but failing miserably as I instinctually glance upwards and come face to face with the handsome state of California.

The striking geographical location smiles wide and sits down at the bar next to us.

"Avocado Shirley Temple," says the state to a bartender, who immediately gets to work fixing California's drink. The geographical location turns to me and extends a hand.

"I'm California," he says with a cool and calm tone.

"Plurk Borden," I tell him.

We shake firmly and then California turns to Jonah, repeating his introduction.

"I'm gonna be honest with you, I came over here to introduce myself because I caught you staring," explains the state. "I don't want you to be embarrassed, though. I just had to tell you that up front."

Jonah and me exchange glances, mortified.

"See, now you're embarrassed," laughs California, "I'm not trying to be a dick here. I'm just honest."

I shake it off, trying to center myself in the presence of such a well-loved state. "No, no, thanks for mentioning something."

"People see celebrities and they never know if it's okay to come and say hello, you know?" California explains. "I just think that it's way better to come right up and get it out of the way, just lay it all out there and let people know that you're a real guy who you can approach and say hello to."

"Well, not everyone's like that," I tell him. "Especially not all states."

"Just the good ones!" California laughs.

"We met Ohio the other day and he was kind of a dick," Jonah ads.

Just then the state's drink arrives, a green swirling beverage that looks absolutely delicious in a manly kind of way.

"So what are you doing all the way out here in Louisiana?" I ask.

The state takes a long sip from his drink, staring out across the pool with a look of quiet contemplation on his face. He seems lost in thought, his mind drifting away to some moment from long, long ago.

"Just had to get out of town for a while," California tells me.

"But don't you have, you know, people to take care of?" I ask. "Where are they all living while you're away?"

"I try not to think about it too much." California tells me. "I mean, I'm sure they're okay. They'll figure it out."

There is an awkward silence for a moment; the three of is sitting and watching people splash about in the cool pool water before us.

"So what's the happening place around here?" asks California. "Where do you guys go for fun?"

"Well, we've got all kinds of clubs in Miami if that's your scene," I tell him.

"Nah," the state says, shaking his head. "I'm looking for something down and dirty; a local dive, you know?"

"There's a bar near Plurk's house that we go to a lot," Jonah suggests, "it's called The Giggling Fingers, right down the street from Thurps Boulevard."

"Thurps Boulevard?" the state yells, spitting out his drink with shock and amazement. "You live down the street from Thurps Boulevard?"

"I do," I tell him, confused by what could possibly be so hilarious about this simple fact.

"That's where I live!" California explains. "What's your address?"

"532 Thurps," I answer.

"This is too crazy, I just moved into 533," yells California, overflowing with excitement at our incredible connection. "What are the chances?"

"One in a million," I tell him, "which means you need to come out with us tonight."

It's a long shot, but I take it.

"I think you're right," says the state with a smile. "Meet you there at ten?"

My heart skips a beat as California says this, shocked that such a well known and handsome celebrity state is interested in hanging out with a couple of common folk like me and my friend. When Jonah and I came to the neighborhood pool on this scorching hot summers day, we had no idea what we'd end up chatting, and especially not making plans, with such an incredible location.

California finishes his drink and then stands up. "Well, I'm gonna go get back into the pool, it's too hot out here. I'll see you guys at ten, though."

"Sounds good," I offer as the state strolls away and then leaps into the water with a beautiful, graceful dive.

Jonah looks over at me, but not with the expression that I was expecting.

"Did that seem kind of… weird to you?" my friend asks.

"If by weird you mean awesome, then yeah it was pretty weird." I scoff.

Jonah struggles to find his words. "What are the chances of him coming to this pool at the same time that we're here, and then approaching us, and then just happening to live right across the street from you?" my friend finally asks.

I shake my head, confused at what exactly Jonah is trying to get at. "So?"

"So… I don't know, it just seems weird," Jonah offers.

We watch as the state does laps back and forth across the pool, enjoying the presence of water that he has been craving so desperately back on the West Coast.

"You're just jealous that he was talking to me more than you," I finally counter.

"Why would I care about that?" Jonah questions.

"Because he's famous and cute," I explain.

Jonah just stares at me blankly. "I don't get it, you're straight."

I scoff. "Please," I tell him, "it doesn't count if it's a state. I'd never bang a dude, but locations are a totally different thing."

"Really?" Jonah counters, skeptically.

"Dude, it's cool if it's between a man and a state of the union, everyone knows that," I tell him.

Jonah finally accepts this and shrugs, then turns back to the bartender. "Can I try one of those Avocado Shirley Temples?"

The bar is quiet tonight; the usual weekend crowd all partied out on this lazy Sunday evening. Me, Jonah and California has found ourselves a booth at the back of the bar and are sharing a bowl of peanuts as we imbibe copious amounts of beer.

California explains to us that these peanuts were harvested on him and we don't believe it, at first, until he shows us the actual location, a beautiful, lush peanut orchard near Redding.

We can't bring our beers to the orchard, but it's beautiful enough to leave them at the bar for a while and take a long walk down the rows and rows of incredible peanut trees, enjoying the warm California air on our skin.

In Redding it is still three hours ahead, so the sunset blooms big and beautiful over our heads, turning the skies above an imperial violet.

"This makes me want to move," Jonah says, "it really is beautiful here."

"Totally," I agree.

"Thanks guys," says the state. "You're making me blush!"

"It's amazing," I tell the celebrity location, laying it on thick, "I just wish we had a better view of the sunset."

I make the sunset remark completely off handedly, not at all request for a change of scenery but simply musing out loud with my own random thought process. California, however, seizes the moment and then the next thing I know we are on the Santa Monica beach, looking out across the seemingly endless expanse of water before us as the sun makes its final exit below the horizon line.

"Whoa," is all that I can say, the word falling limply from my lips.

"It's weird seeing the sun from this side," Jonah observes. "I'm so used to the *sunrise* to being over the water you know?"

California laughs. "Crazy. That's exactly what Plurk said when he was here last year."

The second that these words cross my ears I freeze, glancing over at Jonah to see if he had noticed anything unusual about that sentence, as well. He clearly has, and now the two of us find ourselves in an incredibly awkward situation.

"Well, I think that's all for tonight," I finally say.

Back in the bar, I stand up and shake California's hand, trying to be as casual as I can.

"You guys are out of here?" the state asks.

"Yeah, it's getting pretty late," I tell him.

California looks at his watch. "It's not even midnight yet, you should have another beer!"

"I don't know," Jonah chimes in. "I'm pretty exhausted."

I now notice a strange look working its way across California's face. He seems to have realized something and this new perspective has immediately permeated his entire mood, causing him to tense up significantly.

"You seem like something's wrong," the state says. "Listen, I know that I can come off as a little awkward sometimes but it's just because I never really learned how to talk to people. I was a child star, you know?"

I listen intently, still not buying the nice guy act. Something is definitely creepy about this costal state of the union.

"Honestly, I wanted to come out here to find myself, because I knew that situations like this make me uncomfortable," California explains. "I knew that I was going to have a hard time finding friends and… I remembered you visiting and you seemed really nice."

I fully expect his admission to send me into a tailspin of discomfort but, instead, something entirely different happens; my heart breaks. I actually find myself feeling a little bad for the guy. He may be a tad bit creepy, but it's also incredibly hard moving to a brand new state entirely on your own.

"But, you didn't *just* come out here because of me did you?" I ask, bluntly. "I mean, I don't even know you."

California shakes his head and laughs. "No, of course not! I have other friends in Miami."

I can tell that Jonah is still significantly creeped out, but despite my better judgment I sit back down into the booth. Besides, California *is* a celebrity and the longer we hang out that crazier of a story this will make.

I let out a long sigh. "Alright, one more drink."

California smiles, clearly pleased as he orders us another round.

Two hours later and we all find ourselves stumbling home, making the short walk back towards Thurps Boulevard together with alcohol on our breath and sleep on our minds. I'm utterly exhausted after finding myself on edge the whole night, attempting to balance the discomfort I felt from California's subtle creepiness with the aching attraction that I was simultaneously developing for the state.

It was definitely a brain vs. dick situation, and right now my brain was taking a pummeling.

When we finally get to our houses, the group of us begins to part ways, Jonah heading to his car while me and the Golden State stand talking for a moment. We wave to Jonah as he strolls over to his car, clearly a lot more sober than California and me at this point.

Before he leaves, Jonah flashes me a slightly concerned look but I brush it off, honestly starting to greatly suspect that he is nothing more than jealous of attention I've been receiving from this handsome celebrity location.

"So are you all moved in over there?" I ask California, the taillights of Jonah's car disappearing off into the distance.

"Yeah," he says. "I mean, I'm a state so I don't really have that much stuff as far as furniture goes."

"Cool, cool." I reply, trailing off.

The state cracks a wry grin, clearly thinking something mischievous. "You wanna come over and check the place out?"

"Oh no," I reply, "it's getting late, I better hit the hay."

"You sure?" California says. "Come on, just a night cap to top it off."

I hesitate, my brain swimming with all of the possible outcomes from this unexpected but thrilling night out.

"Alright," I finally relent. "One more drink."

"Great!" California shouts, turning back towards his house and making his way across the street with excitement.

I follow behind, my heart already thumping in my chest at the possible gay encounter that could be looming in the near future between me and this majestic state.

California walks up the front steps of his house and then unlocks his door, letting it swing open into the darkness of the living room.

"Go on in," the state says in a way that sends a strange chill down my spine. Something is wrong here.

"Me first?" I ask, slightly confused by his request.

"Yeah, sure," replies California. "I'm right behind you."

Slowly, I take a step inside, and then another, and another, until I am standing completely within California's house. There is nothing but darkness all around me.

Behind me, the front door squeaks closed, completely removing even the slightest sliver of light.

"Uh, what's going on?" I ask, my voice trembling.

I can hear the door lock somewhere in the black void behind me.

Suddenly, the living room light flips on and I gasp aloud, shocked at the incredible scene that is laid out before me.

Like California had said, the room itself is completely void of any furniture, as bare as can be while a single overhead light illuminates the space with a stark whiteness. The walls, however, are a different story, completely covered with photographs that stretch across every inch of free space, floor to ceiling.

Instinctually, I step forward and lean in closer towards the photographs, finding them to be exactly what I had dreaded; candid pictures of myself.

I scan the wall, finding snapshots that date all the way back to my California trip several years ago, and leading up to as recent as earlier today at the pool.

"I've been following you," says California, a strange blankness in his voice.

"You've been stalking me," I counter, turning around to face him.

The state doesn't refute me on this, just stares daggers into my soul as we stand off on either side of this large empty living room.

"I'm sure you think this is really creepy and weird," the Golden State offers, "but I can explain."

I say nothing; just listen.

"Ever since that trip you took to Los Angeles, I haven't been able to shake the craving to have you near me, to have you inside of me," California professes. "You left and I just felt so empty on my own. The truth is, people come to stay in me for vacations all the time, but I've never met anyone like you Plurk."

My heart slamming in my chest, I suddenly realize that, despite California's strange way of showing it, I feel exactly the same way.

"This is so crazy," is all that I can say, unable to fully understand the emotions that are coursing through me.

Just hours ago I was a regular bro looking for chicks to pick up at the pool, and now everything has completely changed. I feel as though my entire life has been turned upside down.

California slowly begins to step towards me. "Now that you know what it's like to be inside me," the state says, "I can't help but wonder what it would be like to be inside of you."

Suddenly, we are right up next to each other, California's absolutely massive geographical body pressed up seductively against mine. I can feel his mountains and valleys, his rivers and forests, deserts and incredibly toned abs. Without thinking, I lean in and kiss my stalker on the mouth, a surge of sensual energy flowing between us and causing my dick to quickly harden within my pants.

"I want you so bad," I confess to the state. "I don't care if you're a stalker, your golden shores and incredible calves are more than worth it."

We continue to kiss passionately until finally I just can't take it any longer and, overwhelmed with emotion, I drop down to my knees before the majestic location.

I can see his enormous cock rising before me, lifting right up out of his midsection from somewhere near Sacramento. I gasp in astonishment as it grows bigger and bigger until finally the entire length of his massive rod sits inches away from my eager lips.

Not wasting any time, I open wide I let the state slip into my mouth, graciously taking him deep within me.

California let's out a long moan and begins to push farther and farther down, clearly enjoying the sensation as I reach up and gently cradle his balls with one hand. With the other, I wrap my fingers tightly around the base of his shaft and then begin to bob up and down across his length in slow, deliberate movements.

I can feel the Golden State's muscle's tense and release as I move, his entire body grappling with the pleasure that he has been craving for so long. I can only imagine what this must be like for him to finally be intimate with the object of his obsession.

Eventually, I grab California by the hips and pull him forward, forcing his rod as far down my throat as he can possibly go. I'm not exactly ready for his entirety, though, and quickly find myself coughing and gasping as the state removes himself from my mouth.

It takes me a moment to catch my breath, spit hanging from my lips as I look up at my handsome lover, but soon enough I am ready to go once again, opening wide and consuming the state's cock in a stunning deep throat.

This time I'm ready for him, somehow relaxing enough to take California all the way down into the very bottom of my depths. He slides past my gag reflex without any problems, eventually ending up with his hanging balls pressed tightly against my chin and my face pressed hard into his toned, chiseled abs.

California puts his hands against the back of my head and holds me here for a good while, truly savoring the sensation of being full consumed until I just can't take it anymore I have to come up for air.

"Fuck, I love sucking off your southwestern United States dick," I admit, "and I'm not even gay."

"Neither am I, dude," admits the handsome state. "It's not gay if it's between a state and a man. Everybody knows that."

"Right on," I say, nodding with excitement, "right on."

At this point I turn around and fall down onto my hands and knees, popping my ass out towards him and giving it a cute wiggle.

The state watches me with a deep and overwhelming desire in his eyes, focused on the shape of my muscular buns as I present it to him so brazenly.

"You wanna pound me up the butthole?" I coo playfully. "Does this horny state want to plow me up the ass with his big fat coastal cock?"

California nods, and then slaps my ass hard. His flirty punishment causes me to yelp in surprise, but turns me on much more than I ever would have expected. With a total landmass of one hundred and sixty thousand square miles, his size absolutely dwarfs me by comparison, and the submissive aspect of our lop-sized comparison turns me on beyond belief.

As I look back over my shoulder at the state I can feel his thick rod teasing the edges of my back door, testing the limits of my puckered asshole with the head of his shaft.

"Just do it!" I scream. "Just shove that fat fucking dick in there!"

The next thing I know, California is ramming forward hard, stretching the limits of my tightness with his utterly enormous cock. The sensation of his penetration fills me completely with equal parts pain and pleasure, but as the state pulses slowly in and out of my body the ache eventually gives away to a pleasant fullness unlike anything I have ever known.

Immediately, I reach down between my legs and begin to stroke myself off, beating my dick to the rhythm of the state's movements within me.

The pulse of his topographical hips gaining speed, I find myself overwhelmed with pleasure as the orgasmic sensations build in tiny waves within. They start inconspicuous enough, a blossoming heat that simmers deep within and then slowly but surly expands outward, down my arms and legs in an incredible, tingling ecstasy.

With every consecutive wave the feeling grows more and more intense until finally I'm hovering dangerously close to the edge, just about ready to blow my load all over the living room floor before me.

California, however, has other ideas.

Suddenly the state pulls out of me and flips me over onto my back, grabbing me by either leg and pulling them up towards my head so that my asshole is totally exposed. My cock juts out from my torso in all of its aching glory, ready for me to beat myself off while the Golden State continues to rail my already reamed asshole into oblivion.

"Oh my fucking god!" I cry out as California impales me once more, still not quite accustomed to his incredible size.

Now on my back, I watch in awe as California slams up inside of me, his acre's long cock seeming to magically disappear within my body. I am completely at his whim, a man and a state locked within the heat of passion as my rock hard dick bobs wildly in the air against every thrust up my rear.

It's not long before I can feel the aching prostate orgasm start to build once again within me, filling my entire being with a strange and pleasant warmth that moves me to my very core.

I start to cry with happiness, tears streaming down my face. When I look up at California he is crying too, huge tears of joy cascading down along the Redwood Forest and through his desert landscape below like some kind of great biblical flood.

We have finally found each other, the most unlikely pair that one could ever imagine proving that, somehow, love always finds a way. Before tonight there was a hole in my heart that I wasn't even aware of, a vague emptiness that hovered above my life like a dark cloud. Now I know that there's another world out there, another place where the Golden State and me can be together forever.

California reaches down and grabs onto my dick like a giant, fleshy joystick, pumping his hand across my length in time with the rams of his engorged shaft up my asshole. The pleasure is almost immediately overwhelming, a powerful sensation of ecstasy that consumes every sense in my body. I am quaking hard, convulsing with spastic waves of orgasm that roll through me from head to toe and cause several massive payloads of jizz to eject from my cock.

"I'm cumming so hard!" I cry out, California not letting up for a second until I finally collapse back onto the floor in a blissed out haze.

The state pulls his thick rod out of me and begins to beat off furiously above, ready to explode with his own torrent of milky seed.

"Do it!" I command. "Shoot that hot stalker load all over my body!"

I suddenly find myself inside of my new lover, standing on the city streets of San Diego while a cascade of pearly spunk comes spilling across the landscape towards me. I can see it for miles, a tidal wave of stately jizz that nearly blocks out the sun with its incredible presence, uprooting trees and knocking over buildings that stand in it's way.

I barely have enough time to react, turning and running just two steps before the liquid hits me hard and overtakes me, sweeping me off of my feet in a salty cascade of sperm. I'm drowning in it, struggling to stay afloat in the undertow until finally I just don't have the strength to go on and sink beneath the waves.

The next thing I know, I'm back on the floor of California's house, covered in his cum.

The state helps me up and walks me over to the nearby bathroom, where he turns on the shower and sets out two towels. We climb inside together.

The warm water feels incredible against my skin, washing me clean of all the sweat and sperm and giving me a wholesome feeling of freshness once more. I turn around in the water to face California and give him a deep, passionate kiss on the lips.

"I'm sorry I was so creeped out at first," I tell him, pulling away and looking deep into the state's eyes. "It's not every day you get someone following you across the country and secretly taking hundreds of photos that you're not aware of."

"Thousands," California informs me, "but whose counting?"

I shake my head in disbelief, not from the strangeness of this encounter, but at the incredible love that I feel for the great state.

"So what now?" I ask him, the water cascading off of our bodies in two glorious waterfalls.

"I don't ever want you to ever be away from me," California admits.

"I don't want that either," I tell him.

The state wraps his arms around me and pulls me close, enveloping me into his hills and valleys, his glorious coastlines and his sprawling metropolises. I can feel myself sinking deeper and deeper as I lose all sense of spatial relativity.

"Where do you want to live?" California asks. "Los Angeles? Oakland? San Jose?"

"I don't care," I murmur as I disappear completely.

6 THE CURSE OF BIGFOOT BUTT CAMP

I'll admit that the words "adult summer camp" are laughable on the surface. After all, there is a reason we eventually grow up and stop traipsing around in the woods, doing crafts and pitching tents.

That reason is real world responsibility. It might be fun to spend a weekend telling ghost stories around a roaring campfire, but it's not the easiest thing to fit into one's adult schedule.

Some things, however, are worth the vacation days.

I first hear about Bigfoot Butt Camp from my friend, Jeff, who would also be attending his first year out in the woods with me.

"Dude, they have a giant trampoline, and a zip line. If you don't come you're gonna regret it." My coworker says.

I laugh to myself as I take in Jeff's excitement from across the table. We're in a diner next door to the office, taking our lunch break over a shared BLT and a plate of fries. "I don't know, man." I tell him. "I'm gonna pull my back out on that thing or something, I'm too old now."

"You're twenty five." Jeff informs me, rolling his eyes. "We're still very young, you know."

"But not summer camp young." I counter.

"That's the point!" Jeff says. "Why should they have all of the fun? Look at us working day in, day out at the office; slaving away for rent, a car payment, a new fucking suit. How great would it be if all we had to worry about for a week was whether or not we'd earn our fishing merit badge?"

"They have badges?" I question.

"They have everything." Jeff tells me.

I think about this for a moment, considering whether a weekend off in the woods with my friend sounds better than the trip I had already planned to Mexico. I shrug; the beach can wait.

"Alright, I'll go." I tell him. "But to be honest, I just want to hang out with some bigfeet."

Even though the bigfeet have been mostly integrated into our culture at this point, seeing them in the flesh is still something of a rarity. I can't imagine what it would be like to spend a whole week with the majestic creatures up close, instead of just a few limited interactions on my way too and from work.

"Have you ever hung out with a bigfoot?" Asks Jeff.

"Not really." I tell him. "I had a meeting with one from the New York division the other day but the rest of his team did most of the talking. There's one living a few doors down at my apartment building too, but I rarely see him."

"You know they say Senator Yuldok is going to run for president this year." Jeff informs me. "Can you imagine that? A bigfoot as president."

I take a long sip from my drink. The whole idea really does sound too crazy to be true, but it's a brand new world that we live in.

"Yeah, it's nuts." I finally tell him.

Bigfoot Butt Camp is located deep in the Oregon wilderness, far removed from the hustle and bustle city life that I've grown accustomed to. It's actually a little intimidating to be out here in a place that still seems to belong to these once mythical creatures, instead of spotting one riding the bus or shopping for groceries. There is something about the confines of an urban setting that has robbed these modern bigfeet of their sublime, natural beauty.

Jeff and I pull my SUV up to a large wooden gate that restricts access to the remainder of the desolate dirt road. There is a massive sign hanging above us that has been constructed from lashed branches, spelling out the words Bigfoot Butt Camp in jagged wood. Below, and just off the side of the road, is a tall hut from which a bigfoot slowly emerges. The beast walks over to our car as I roll down the driver's side window.

"Welcome to camp, boys!" The bigfoot says with a wide smile. He reaches out his utterly humungous hand and we shake. "Just go ahead and drive down to your left. Head towards the lake, there's gonna be parking right there. We've got a bonfire going already so just find a seat and the opening ceremony will start in about twenty minutes."

I nod. "Thanks."

The bigfoot heads back into his hut and seconds later the gate is swinging open to allow us entry.

I turn to Jeff. "Okay, fine. This is fucking awesome."

Jeff laughs.

We travel a short distance along the rest of the dirt road until the thick forest opens up into a beautiful view of Abs Lake, which stretches out before us in all of its picturesque glory.

I park the car and step out into the fresh air, taking a deep breath as I close my eyes and lean my head back. The afternoon sun is pleasant against my skin, and it suddenly hits me just how rarely I find myself out from under the shadow of a tall building while back in the big city.

"You gonna just stand there are day, Ken?" Jeff asks me with a laugh.

I open my eyes. "You were right, I did need to get out of town." I tell him.

Jeff grabs my bag from the trunk of the SUV and hands it to me, then throws his own over his shoulder. My friend gives me a solid pat on the back, "I know." He says with a smile.

Without much time before the introductory bonfire, Jeff and I forgo setting up in our designated tent spot and, instead, head directly towards the opening ceremony to grab a seat. The walk is not far.

Soon enough, we find ourselves in a large clearing the overlooks Lake Abs in all of its smooth, reflective glory. There is a raging fire out front while a set of elevated benches make their way around the outer rim, already packed with excited men just who are buzzing with anticipation for the weekend.

Jeff and me find a seat near the back. Seconds later, a large bigfoot in shorts and an official looking button up comes walking out from the forest and stands before the bonfire. His presence settles the crowd almost immediately, and soon enough the entire ritual becomes dead silent, save for the crackles and pops that emit from the large fire pit.

"Who's ready for a good time?" The handsome bigfoot counselor asks in his loud, booming voice.

Our crowd of young professionals bursts into a raucous applause.

"That's what I like to hear!" Continues the counselor. "How many of you work in an office?"

A majority of the crowd raises their hands.

The bigfoot nods. "Well, this is our office." He says confidently, swinging an arm out behind him. "And for the next week, it's your office, too. We want you to forget about the stress of the outside world and live in the moment while you're here at Bigfoot Butt Camp. "

A handful of other bigfeet suddenly emerge from the surrounding wilderness and stand before us, all clad in the same uniform. They are a shockingly handsome bunch, and although I've never been sexually attracted to another man before, their impeccable sasquatch features are hard to deny.

"My name is Rim Barkoon." Announces our speaker. "Over the next week you'll get to know me quite well, along with all of the other counselors. If you see anyone in this uniform then we are here to help you."

Jeff leans over to me and speaks in a hushed tone. "Dude, is it just me or is Rim kinda… hot?"

I shake my head in amazement. "I was thinking the same thing. I mean, they're all pretty hot."

"Does that make us gay?" Jeff jokes.

I laugh. "I don't think so, man."

Rim Barkoon steps out in front of his fellow counselors now, his voice immediately taking on a more serious tone. "Now, we are going to have a lot of fun this weekend, I promise you that, but we have something a little serious to address here right off of the bat."

Rim scans the crowd with his eyes, making sure that every single one of us is giving our full attention to the message he's about to deliver.

"We plan these camps the best that we can, but every once in a while they end up on the evening of a full moon. That's our bad." Rim admits, putting a hand up. "I could give you some kind of excuse about the moon colonization throwing things off, but we should have known better. You've already paid for a full week so we will be cutting one day off your total bill, but all of tonight's activities have been canceled."

Concerned chatter suddenly erupts through our crowd.

"I know, I know." Says Rim. "But this is very important for everyone's safety. All of the councilors here have a very specific medical condition that will only be an issue tonight during the full moon. During that time, we need every one of you to say in your tents? Is that understood?"

Jeff suddenly raises his hand. I glance over at him, utterly mortified as I try to get him to pull it down. Before I can, however, the handsome, muscular bigfoot has spotted him.

"Yes, you there." Says Rim.

Jeff stands up. "Hi, I was just wondering if you could tell us what this medical condition is? Is it dangerous? Can humans catch it?"

Rim exchanges glances with the rest of the mythical creatures before us. Finally, his gaze returns to Jeff. "I understand your concern, I really do, which is why we are offering free refunds to anyone who wants to leave now. To answer your question; No, humans can't catch this, but there are other issues to be concerned about. Regardless, if you stay in your tent you will absolutely not be harmed. That's a guarantee."

Jeff seems satisfied with this answer and sits back down.

"What's the medical condition?" Someone else shouts from the crowd. "Just tell us."

"Unfortunately, I can't tell you exactly what this medical condition is, thanks to the Bigfoot Human Integration Act of two thousand and sixteen." Explains Rim. "If anyone would like to receive their refund, they can leave now. We have an assistant counselor waiting in the parking lot who can help you with that."

A handful of campers stand up and make their way down from the wooden benches, heading back towards the lot.

Jeff leans in towards me. Are you scared?"

His words enter my ears but somehow get lost before reaching my brain. Instead, my focus is utterly singular, my eyes gazing upon the gorgeous visage of Rim Barkoon. The bigfoot is unlike anyone I have every laid eyes on, and the longer that I stare, the more deeply in love I fall with this majestic creature of the forest. He is the perfect combination of down home good looks and a bad boy, bigfoot attitude. I'm hooked, and I'm definitely not going anywhere.

"Are you scared?" Jeff repeats. "Ken?"

I finally shake my head. "Nah man, I'm excited for the week. Who cares about one night stuck in our tent?"

Jeff shrugs, nodding in agreement. "What's the worst that could happen?"

There is a rumor going around camp at the bigfeet are all vampires, and that when the full moon rises they will immediately turn into bloodthirsty bats.

"Ridiculous." I tell Jeff, who sits in the tent across from me as we play Go Fish by the light of our small, battery-powered lantern. "Vampires don't come out on a full moon."

"Yes, they do!" Jeff assures me.

I shake my head. "Don't you mean mummies?"

Jeff looks up from his cards, deathly serious. "Are you fucking with me?"

"Yes." I tell him. "Everyone knows that mummies aren't real. They probably just have some kind of bigfoot disease that we humans don't know about."

Suddenly, a long, drawn-out moan cuts through the forest around us. Jeff and I freeze, staring directly into each other's fearful expressions as our ears strain against the following silence.

"Did you hear that?" Jeff finally asks.

I nod.

"Didn't that sound like a mummy to you?" My friend continues, his voice trembling.

"There's no such thing as mummies." I whisper to Jeff. "It's just some kind of animal or something."

"What kind of animal makes a sound like that?" Jeff counters.

We sit in silence for a moment until finally my friend begins to crawl over to the front flap of the tent.

"What are you doing?" I ask, shocked.

"I'm gonna go check it out." Jeff tells me.

"Are you kidding me?" I respond, unable to process his assertion. "Did you not hear the rules? We need to stay here in our tents all night, no exceptions."

Jeff rolls his eyes. "Come on buddy, live a little. Don't you want to figure out what's going on?"

"Let's just finish the card game, okay?" I beg, my fear getting the best of me.

My friend cracks a mocking smile. "I'll be right back."

The next thing that I know, Jeff has unzipped the flap and slipped out into the darkness. I can hear his footsteps crunching off into the distance as he steps farther and farther away from the tent, eventually disappearing completely.

I listen hard for any signs of life. Nothing. The only sounds are resonating internally as my heart pounds hard within my chest.

"Jeff?" I finally ask, already knowing that he's much to far away to hear me or answer back.

I am all alone.

I sit frozen like this for much longer than I realize, my thoughts swimming with every different possibility of what could have happened to my friend. With every minute that passes by I grow more and more anxious until finally I'm a trembling ball of nerves, desperate for any kind of answer that I can find in this utterly harrowing situation.

I crawl to the edge of the tent and slowly unzip the flap, popping my head out and staring through the dimly lit trees. The only light is that from the moon above, casting the surroundings in a strange and eerie glow.

"Jeff!" I hiss. "Stop fucking around!"

As expected, I get nothing in response.

Finally, I've had enough. I unzip the tent completely and then climb out into the night, slowly letting my eyes adjust to the darkness.

"Jeff!" I call out again, a little louder now. I take one step forward, and then another, and another, until eventually I've left the tent far behind me.

After walking a ways I eventually come to a dirt path that winds up through the forest. I follow it quietly and carefully, my senses on full alert as the branches that crisscross above me sway in the wind.

Suddenly, another long groan slices through the night. I freeze, peering down the path towards where the sound originated. I can just barely make out a large figure standing before me, some twenty feet away.

"Jeff?" I ask.

The figure groans again and begins shambling forward.

"Jeff, knock it off. You know we're not supposed to be out here." I tell him, my voice trembling.

As soon as the figure is close enough to see I gasp aloud, my body freezing in fear. There before me is the handsome head councilor, Rim Barkoon, only he's not the same bigfoot that I first laid eyes on just hours earlier. Instead, the once fresh-faced mythical creature has warped into something strange and undead, a mummy bigfoot wrapped in hanging bandages that staggers through the shining moonlight.

My first instinct is to turn and run, yet something holds me in place. I watch as the creature steps closer and closer until he is right up next to me, which is where I suddenly realize that my trembling has not been out of fear, but arousal.

"You're so fucking sexy." I finally say to Rim.

The bigfoot mummy stops and eyes me hungrily from just a few feet away, his cock growing longer and harder with every passing second. His rod juts out from his body like a massive, third appendage, its sheer size utterly intimidating.

"Suck me." Rim moans.

"But I'm… But I'm…" I stammer, my mind struggling to find an excuse that would allow me to do what my heart so desperately craves. "But I'm straight!"

The mummy cracks a knowing grin and then places a bandaged hand onto my shoulder. "Are you sure about that?"

I consider his words for a moment as my heart skips into double time, my mind reeling from the implications of what stands before me. If I go through with this, there is no turning back.

I take a deep breath.

Slowly, I drop down onto my knees and take Rim's massive shaft into my tight grip, pumping my hand slowly across the length of his hard rod.

The mummy lets out a powerful sigh, his eyes closed as he tilts his head back and savors the sensation of my firm hand job.

"Do you like that?" I coo seductively.

The bigfoot mummy moans loudly in affirmation.

"Then how about this?" I ask. Seconds later, I open my mouth wide and take the creature's shaft within my lips, then begin to pump my head up and down across his length in slow deliberate moments. I find a good pace and eventually begin to speed up, cradling the bigfoot's balls with one hand while I service him orally.

Rim places his hands against the back of my head and guides me along, faster and faster until he is fucking my face with everything that he's got, using me as a filthy human sex toy.

Eventually, I push down as far as I can and hold, taking the bigfoot's incredible rod all the way into my throat where it comes to rest in my depths, completely consumed. I look up at my handsome bigfoot lover, my eyes watering, and give him a playful wink.

When I've finally run out of air I pull back and gasp, releasing Rim's rod and wiping a long stand of saliva from my lips. I stand up and kiss the bigfoot mummy on the mouth, hard, running my hands along his ripped body before leading the beast off of the path towards a nearby stump.

I remove my shirt and toss it off into the forest, then my pants and underwear comes next until I am completely naked, save for my hiking boots. I bend over the remains of this fallen tree and look back at Rim.

"How about you pound this tight gay ass for a while you ripped mummy stud." I say, relentlessly horny for the monster's undead cock.

Rim wastes no time at all, saddling up behind me and aligning his cock with the taut edge of my puckered backdoor. He slaps my ass hard with his massive, hairy hands and then grabs me by the hips, pushing forward into my tightness.

I cry out in a mixture of pain and pleasure, not entirely ready for his enormous size as my body struggles to accommodate his dick. I am stretched to my limits.

Rim begins to pump in and out of my rectum; my entire body reacting to every aching thrust from the strange beast. A shudder runs down the length of my spine and my eyes roll back into my head as I brace myself for his pounds.

"Oh fuck, that cock is so fucking huge!" I tell my handsome monster lover. "I don't know if I can take it!"

"You can take it." Rim assures me confidently.

Eventually, the pace of the bigfoot mummy's pumps has increased into a merciless slam, but with every thrust my asshole relaxes until, eventually, the pain disappears completely and I find myself in a world of blissed out fullness. I reach down between my legs and grab ahold of my hanging shaft, beating myself off to the rhythm of Rim's pounding.

"Oh my god, you're gonna make me blow much fucking load so hard." I hiss through clenched teeth.

Rim smiles. "Not so fast."

The next thing I know the creature is spinning me around and taking me into his bandaged arms. Rim lifts me up into the air and I wrap my muscular legs around him, still dwarfed my the massive size of this undead creature.

Rim reaches down and maneuvers his cock into position, then eventually lowers me onto his length, impaling my asshole with his huge rod.

"Oh shit!" I call out into the dark forest, still not entirely accustomed to the bigfoot's enormity.

"You're so tight." The bigfoot mummy moans.

I grab onto Rim's shoulders as he begins to raise and lower me, using the power of gravity to slam me even harder than before. With every plunge downward an overload of sensation floods through me, eliciting feelings I could have never before dreamed of back when I considered myself a straight man.

Soon my bigfoot lover is hammering me with everything that he's got. My body is quaking with spasms of an impending prostate orgasm, unable to contain all of this ecstasy within. I grab ahold of my cock, stroking furiously over the length of my shaft as I tilt my head back and let out an incredible howl, the sound drifting off into the fresh night air.

"I'm cumming!" I scream.

Immediately, a powerful wave of sensation hits me, pulsing though my body hard as a blast of jizz erupts from the head of my cock. It splatters between Rim and I, covering our sweaty muscular bodies with spunk.

Rim is following right behind me, and within seconds he has lifted me up off of his dick and placed me onto the ground below him. I lay out in the ferns, looking up at the powerful creature as he beats his rod above me.

"Do it!" I command. "Cover me in for bigfoot mummy seed! I need your jizz all over me!"

Rim does as he's told, letting out a powerful cry and then ejecting a massive payload of milky white cum across my face and chest. It rains down onto me in a series of splatters that paint my skin with pearly liquid.

"That's good." I coax. "That's real good."

When the bigfoot finally finishes, he stumbles back against a tree to catch his breath.

"That was amazing." I tell him in a cock drunk haze.

There is no response. I glance over to see that the creature has disappeared off into the forest from which it came.

When I've finally collected my sense I stand up and gather my clothes, then make my way down to the water of the lake. I take off my hiking boots on the shore and wade out into the cool and refreshing water, floating along the surface as I stare up at the full moon that hangs in the sky overhead.

When I return to my tent, Jeff is nowhere to be found.

The next morning I find that my friend is still missing and immediately start to panic. I throw open the flap of my tent and climb out, looking around for any signs of his return while I slept.

"Jeff!" I call. "Jeff!"

A follow camper walks over and asks me if everything is all right.

"I don't know what happened to my friend." I tell him, unable to hide the desperation in my voice. "He left last night and he hasn't come back."

The other camper shakes his head. "That's no good." The man says. "You better tell a councilor."

Flooded with concern, I immediately head down the path towards the main cabin.

"Hey!" I call out as I arrive, grabbing the attention of the nearest bigfoot. "I think my friend is missing."

The bigfoot counselor, immediately takes me inside the building, which has been outfitted as some kind of woodsy, all-purpose office. The creature walks around his desk and sits down in front of a computer, while I find a seat on the other side.

"Alright, what is your friend's name, and when was the last time you saw him?" The councilor asks.

"His name is Jeff…" I start, trailing off. "Jeff… something."

The bigfoot glances at me skeptically. "You don't know your friends last name?"

I nod. The fact that I don't know Jeff's last name strikes me as odd, as well, but I suppose it's just something I'd just never really considered until now.

"And when was the last time you saw him?" The bigfoot continues. "Typing a few things into his computer."

"Last night." I explain. "We were in our tent and he heard a noise. He went out to see what it was and he never came back."

The bigfoot counselor stares at me with a grave concern. "You know that you weren't supposed to leave your tent during the full moon."

"I know." I tell him. "I tried to stop him." Of course, I neglect to mention that I, too, followed Jeff out into the forest.

The bigfoot types a few more things into his computer and then slaps the spacebar. He stares at the screen for a moment before turning back to me. "Is this some kind of joke?" The bigfoot asks.

I shake my head. "No, why?"

"There is no record of any Jeff checking in to camp." The bigfoot councilor informs me. "And if I recall, you arrived here alone."

I'm utterly confused. "No, I came here with my friend Jeff."

The bigfoot lets out a long sigh and then finally turns away from me and opens up a large cabinet. "Let's just consult the All Seeing Eye, shall we?"

Moments later, the bigfoot pulls out a small, glass box from the cabinet and places it onto the desk between us. Within the square box is what appears to be a human eye, which floats around in a translucent liquid.

Suddenly, the eye swivels around to look directly at me. I jump. "Whoa! What is that?"

"I just told you." The bigfoot replies. "The All Seeing Eye. It knows everything."

"That's incredible." I exclaim. "Why do you keep it in the cabinet?"

The bigfoot gives me an irritated look and ignores my question. "All Seeing Eye." He asks. "Why does my friend here think that Jeff checked into camp with him?"

The eye is silent for a moment, and then suddenly a strange voice erupts through my subconscious mind via telepathic speech. "Jeff is a manifestation of your latent gayness." The eye informs me. "He does not exist in reality."

"What?" I ask, understanding the words but unable to accept the truth behind them.

"Jeff is a figment of your imagination, more specifically your repressed homosexuality. He brought you here because you could not do it yourself, and now that you've turned gay there is no longer any use for Jeff." The eye explains.

"I'm gay now?" I ask, shocked.

"Yes." The eye tells me. "Incredibly gay."

The bigfoot councilor smiles and lifts up the All Seeing Eye, placing it back into the filing cabinet. "Anything else I can help you with?" He asks.

I shake my head and stand up. "No, I'm sorry to bother you."

"It's no worry." The counselor says, suddenly sympathetic to my situation. "This kind of learning experience is exactly what Bigfoot Butt Camp is all about."

7 REAMED BY MY REACTION TO THE TITLE OF THIS BOOK

A familiar but sharp ringing cuts through my headset, and I immediately reach up to press the "answer call" button.

"Hello, this is Josh Gorpin, Blue's Brownies Incorporated." I say, leaning back into my chair and giving myself a spin. Spinning is one of the few luxuries that I have here in this cramped cubicle.

"Josh, it's Peter." Comes the voice on the other end.

I roll my eyes. "Dude, why do you keep distracting me? I've got so much work to get done today before five."

"Oh shit." Peter offers. "Sorry man, I was just kind of bored over here."

Peter and I are both hard workers with comfortable salary jobs, but I often find myself being very jealous of the relaxed environment at his office, which just happens to be located a few miles east of my own looming high rise.

This company has a more traditional work environment, while Peter seems to have all the time in the world to send me goofy emails and completely inappropriate attachments.

"Did you check out that link I sent you?" Peter continues.

"Yeah." I tell him, maximizing my email and staring at the pixelated message that sits unopened on my screen. "Well, I mean no, I didn't open it."

"Why not?" Peter cries out.

"Dude, you wrote 'not safe for work' in the title and then sent it over to me while you know I'm at work." I explain, slightly frustrated. "You're gonna get me fired."

"Oh god, no I'm not." Peter counters, mockingly.

"You're not even supposed to be calling me on this line, this is my work phone." I continue.

"Yeah, but on this line you get to use your headset and I know how much you like that." My friend says with a laugh.

I know that he's just messing with me, but Peter is actually correct about the headphone thing so I let it slide. As ridiculous as it sounds, talking on the headset feels pretty bad ass.

"So what is it?" I ask. "I'm not going to open it at work so you might as well just tell me."

Peter sighs. "Well, it's better if you just look at it, but fine. Do you know who Buck Trungle is?"

I begin to flip a pencil up into the air and catch it as we talk. "Nope. Tell me."

"An author." Peter explains. "Like..."

I stop throwing the pencil. "Like?"

Peter sighs. "This sucks trying to explain. You kind of just have to look at the covers of his books. They're crazy."

"Crazy how?" I continue to prod.

"Like super weird and totally gay." Peter tells me.

"Why would I want to look at gay book covers?" I question. "I'm straight."

"Hey, me too!" Peter protests, "But they're so funny dude, you've gotta check them out. One is called *Space Raptor Butt Invasion.*"

I can't help up laugh. "Seriously? Raptor like the dinosaur?"

"Yes!" Peter shouts. "There's a bunch about dinosaurs, and unicorns, too. There's even one about fucking a plane called *I'm Gay For My Billionaire Jet Plane*!"

"Is he for real?" I ask.

"I don't know." Peter admits. "I mean, it seems like he is but its kind of hard to tell sometimes. Like, this new book... I don't even know what to say about it."

There is something strange is Peter's tone as he tells me this, a powerful weight to his words that sets me ever so slightly on edge.

"What's the name of the new book?" I ask.

There is silence on the other end of the line. I wait for a brief moment and then try again. "Peter, what's the name of the new book?"

"Oh, sorry." My friend suddenly apologizes, ripped back into reality from whatever spaced out zone he was just occupying. "I think you should check it out for yourself."

"Dude, just tell me." I protest.

"It's in the link." Peter counters, an odd flatness in his voice. "Hey, I've gotta go."

"You have to go?" I scoff. "What, did someone finally give you something to do over there?"

The line abruptly goes dead.

"Peter?" I ask. It takes me a moment to realize that he's actually gone and when I finally do I'm not exactly sure what to make of it. Regardless, it's probably for the better because I can finally stop being distracted and get some work done for a change.

I pull my chair back towards my desk and place a stack of papers in front of me, pulling off the top few and then diving in to scan for mistakes. Right now I'm editing internal documents regarding our acquisition of a brand new company; nothing exciting in any way, shape or form, but it's something that has to get done.

Eventually, though, my thoughts begin to wander away from the task at hand, settling on the tiny yellow mail icon that remains unopened on my computer screen.

"Not safe for work." I read aloud.

This type of warning is standard for things forwarded around in an environment like mine, a not so subtle suggestion to save it until you get home. The problem, however, is that it's so fucking vague. Does it mean that the content inside is hardcore pornography, or just some silly joke with a little swearing?

I drag my mouse's arrow across the computer screen, letting it hover above the unopened letter from Peter as my heart rate quickens. Might as well live a little, I think to myself.

I'm just about to click, when suddenly my phone rings through my headset once again. I reach up and click the button to talk. "Hello, this is Josh Gorpin, Blue's Brownies Incorporated."

"Josh!" Peter shouts loudly into my ears, causing me to wince. I can immediately tell that something is wrong.

"What's going on over there?" I ask my friend.

Peter ignores my question. "Josh, whatever you do, don't open the email."

"What?" I question, not exactly sure if I heard him correctly.

"Whatever you do, do not open that email I sent you." Peter repeats.

I notice now that there is an unusual amount of noise in the background of Peter's office, a cacophony of sounds making their way through the receiver. It sounds like a mixture of violent shouting and long, low groans.

"Dude, what's going on over there?" I ask.

"Josh, just listen to me." Peter says again, his voice growing frantic. "Oh shit…"

Suddenly, the line goes dead again, prompting me to finally conclude that this entire thing has been some kind of tasteless practical joke.

I'm about to open the email when suddenly I'm interrupted yet again by Raxlo, the head of human resources, who appears in the doorway of my cubicle.

"Hey, Josh." Raxlo starts. "There's a forward going around about this Buck Trungle guy, do you know what I'm talking about?"

I freeze abruptly, then slowly spin in my chair to face Raxlo. I hesitate before answering, not exactly sure if I should admit to anything at this point. Eventually, I decide to play my hand close to the chest.

"Oh, no I don't." I tell him, playing dumb. "Who's that?"

"God." Raxlo says, straight faced.

I eye him up and down, trying to discern if he's fucking with me or not, but despite Raxlo's awkwardness he appears to be genuine in his answer.

"God?" I ask.

Raxlo nods. "To me and you, yes. Not to them out there."

I'm utterly confused, but I decide to simply nod in response. "Okay. Well, I don't know him."

"You can go home early then." Raxlo informs me. "Everyone else is having a meeting in the conference room."

"Are you serious?" I question, but Raxlo leaves before I can even get the words out of my mouth.

I stand up from my chair and look around the rest of the office, noticing now that well over half of the employees have stood, as well, and are now making their way to the main conference room.

Sufficiently creeped out, I reach down and grab my bag, then begin heading towards the elevator.

Already within the conference room, I can see a handful of my coworkers undressing in front of the large paned windows, but the second we make eye contact one of them walks over and draws the blinds.

Something is definitely wrong here, but for the life of me I just can't seem to put my finger on it. Instead, I find myself panicking, trying to calm myself as I ride the elevator down to the first floor and then heading out into our office's parking lot. My heart is slamming in my chest, my senses on high alert as I climb into my ride and pull out onto the street.

"Holy shit!" I suddenly cry out as I swerve to avoid two twenty-something men who are standing right in the middle of the road. I hit the breaks and look back in my rear view mirror, ready to start apologizing profusely until I realize that they are completely oblivious of me and my big, loud car.

Instead, the men are locked in the troughs of passion, fucking each other with reckless abandon in the middle of the street. Their pants are around their ankles as they slam into one another, crying out with unbridled passion.

I throw my car back into drive and continue on my way.

By now I've begun to notice other couples, and sometimes more, slamming into each other without a care in the world. It makes absolutely no sense, especially when I realize the strange coincidence that all of these illicit pairings are gay.

There are very few other cars on the street, and the handful of other drivers that I see seem just as confused as I am, terrified looks plastered across their faces as they attempt to navigate through this surreal, new world.

I reach down and flip on the radio, hoping to find some information about whatever's going on.

"He really is an incredible author." Says a female announcer. "And with this new book, Buck Trungle has finally skyrocketed into the mainstream."

"I'll say." Responds the announcer's male counterpart. "Some people are starting to call on Dr. Trungle to run for president of the United States, including President Yuldok himself who is, apparently, a big fan of the new book."

"I think we all are." Says the female announcer, laughing.

"Well, to those of you just joining us, I'm Talp Bornin and this is my co-host Hedge Wizarp." The man says. "And we've just entered the second hour of our twenty four hour special on world-renowned author, Buck Trungle."

"Honestly, It's going so well that I think we might want to extend this to a whole week!" Interjects Hedge.

"Or year!" Counters Talp. "To bad we won't be around that long, we're already halfway done!"

"For those of you not already aware, Buck Trungle is the author of such masterpieces as *Pounded By President Bigfoot*, *My Ass Is Haunted By The Gay Unicorn Colonel*, and *Pounded In The Butt By My Own Butt*." Explains Hedge. "The latter of those was hailed as a transhumanist masterpiece and prompted Trungle to follow up with the sequel *Pounded In The Butt By My Book 'Pounded In The Butt By My Own Butt*.'"

"Sounds very meta." Adds Talp.

"Oh, it is." Agrees Hedge. "For those listeners who don't know, 'meta' is a word used to describe anything that is self referential. Things that break the fourth wall and, often, ask the audience themselves to become a participant."

"Ooh, very interesting." Talp says. "And a perfect segue into Dr. Trungle's newest 'Trungler'."

"Yes!" Replies Hedge. "Some are saying that this new book is so meta that it has literally made us start to question our own existence, suggesting that the entire world we live in could literally be a work of erotic fiction."

Both of the anchors laugh simultaneously.

"We have plenty of reports that hearing the title alone will turn you instantly gay." Explains Talp. "Which is why we are going to tell you all about it right now."

Just then I reach my house and pull up into the driveway, turning off my car and hopping out. The street appears empty but I can hear the passionate moans and groans of gay sex echoing across the block. I immediately head inside, locking the door behind me.

Now that I'm here, however, I have no idea what to do with myself. Is the world going to make any more sense from inside my living room?

Will I wake up in the morning and everything is back to normal?

I sit down in front of my television and turn it on, hoping to ease my anxiety and take my mind of the craziness of the outside world, but instead my vision is assaulted by sudden and graphic depictions of gay sex. I scramble to change the channel and quickly realize that every station has been somehow converted into hardcore pornography.

"What the fuck?" I say aloud, finally opting to turn the television off entirely. "What the hell is going on?"

Finally, I just can't take it anymore, I reach over to the coffee table before me and grab my laptop, opening it up and immediately logging into my email. I place my cursor over the unopened letter icon and take a deep breath.

Finally, I click.

The message opens up onto my screen, a few simple sentences followed by a link at the bottom.

"Dude, have you seen this guy?" I read Peter's words aloud. "This shit is so crazy, you've gotta check out the title of his new book."

I click the link below.

Suddenly, a massive book cover appears on my screen, revealing the title, *Reamed By My Reaction To The Title Of This Book* and instantly turning me gay. All of my senses are overwhelmed with a glorious bright light that hums across my entire body, elevating me to a higher plane of consciousness where I become acutely aware that I am nothing more than a character in a short story. On one hand you would think that this would be a terrifying notion, but you must also consider the fact that you, the reader, are also now aware that you're simply a character in an erotic short, and you are not terrified in the least.

Is it simply because you are not ready to accept it yet? Or because you've always known?

I suddenly realize that my eyes have been closed this entire time and when I open them, my reaction to the title is hovering right in front of me, glowing with a beautiful bright light like the whiteness of a book page or this very kindle screen. It has assumed as physical form, an undulating blob of beautiful, explicit gayness that drifts closer and closer to me.

"I can't believe I'm just a character in a book." I finally say.

The reaction simply exists before me, not saying a word but soothing my soul from the inside out. A smile crosses my face.

"I'd love for you to fuck me." I continue.

"Good." Says the reaction. "Because the better you do, the more likely our dear readers will be able to accept that they too, have been turned gay by their reaction to this book. They have no idea that they are figments of Chuck Tingle's imagination, and the sooner that they realize this, the sooner we can all join in harmony."

"I understand." I tell my reaction.

I slip down off of the front of the couch and push back the coffee table, making room for the physical representation of my own emotional state, then reach out and grab his cock firmly in my hand. My reaction is absolutely gorgeous; tan, muscular and sporting an incredible set of abs that has to be seen to be believed.

"You like that?" I ask, playfully.

"You know what I like." Says the reaction. "You know everything about me."

Immediately, I open wide and take the manifestation's rod into my mouth, pumping up and down across the length of his shaft with expert precision. Despite never being with a man before, I suddenly realize that I am a fictional character and can be anything that I want. In fact, before the events of this book, a point at which I did not exist, I decide that I spent hours upon hours in the gym. The next thing I know, I am just as ripped as my reaction is.

I continue to bob my head across my reactions cock with feverish intensity, gradually speeding up until finally I plunge deep and hold, taking his shaft entirely into my mouth in a stunning deep throat. The reaction let's out a long, satisfied moan of pleasure as I hold him there, running my tongue across the bottom of his shaft and tickling his balls.

The reaction's rod is planted firmly in my mouth, my face pressed hard against his incredible, muscular abs. He places his hands against the back of my head, asserting his dominance until finally I'm almost completely out of air and pull back with a loud gasp.

A long strand of saliva hangs down from my lips, providing me just enough lube to beat my reaction off frantically for a moment. I stand abruptly, tearing off my shirt and pants and throwing them to the side. My underwear comes next, and soon enough I'm completely naked in front of this incredible being. The manifestation eyes me up hungrily.

"Do you like what you see?" I coo.

"Yes." The reaction tells me. "Aside from a few spelling errors you've been written perfectly."

I smile and turn around, leaning forward over the couch in front of me and popping my ass out towards my strange new lover. I reach back and grab my ass cheek with one hand, spreading open my puckered hole.

"Ream me." I command.

The reaction positions himself behind me, carefully aligning the head of his shaft with the tightness of my back door and then slowly pushing forward, impaling me with a brutal strength. I grip the back of the couch tightly and brace myself against the reaction's powerful thrusts.

My reaction's cock is absolutely enormous, stretching my tight asshole to its very limits as he plunges in and out of me. The manifestation quickly finds a steady pace, pounding in a perfect rhythm that hits my prostate just right from the inside. I close my eyes tight as a strange pleasure begins to boil within me, starting as an aching simmer and then expanding down my arms and legs as I begin to tremble. I quake with ecstasy, wrapped up in the moment as I reach down between my legs and grab onto my hard, hanging shaft.

"Fuck!" I groan. "I'm so fucking close to blowing this huge load."

"Oh, I'm not finished with you yet." My reaction says, pulling out of my ass abruptly and lifting me up into his massive arms. He turns around and then lays me out across the coffee table, spreading my muscular legs wide as my cock juts out from my body.

My reaction wastes no time getting back to work, pounding away at my maxed out asshole with everything that he's got as I reach down and beat myself off. Then sensation is incredible, a fullness unlike anything I have ever experienced.

"I can't believe my reaction to this book title knows how to fuck me so good!" I cry out.

"Believe it!" The reaction exclaims, driving the point home with his rock hard shaft.

Once more, I begin to approach the wall of a powerful orgasm but, before I can, the reaction has one last surprise.

"Look back." The manifestation says.

I lean my head over the edge of the coffee table so that I'm upside down, staring out behind me.

"Do you see them?" My reaction asks.

"No." I admit.

"Look harder then, you filthy little twink!" The manifestation demands, slapping me hard on the ass.

"All I see is my wall." I tell him.

"Don't look with your eyes." My reaction explains. "Look with your mind. You know that you're not real now, so why would that wall be?"

His words make more sense than I'd like to admit and, almost immediately, I find myself gazing past the wall and through the words on this page, seeing my readers themselves.

"Holy shit, is that who I think it is?" I gasp, my reaction never letting up for a second as he hammers away at my butthole.

"It is." The reaction says. "Now cum for them!"

My entire body begins to quake with an incredible pleasure, sending spastic convulsions of bliss up and down my spine. I bite my lip, tears rolling down my cheeks as I grapple with the intense joy and strange hollowness of realizing that, as soon as you stop reading this, I will cease to exist. Moments later, I cum harder than I ever have, screaming out with a howl that can be heard for miles upon miles around us. I sound vibrates through the letters on this very page.

I am leaving my body, splitting into a million pieces as I change form into something completely unknown that travels out across the universe in every direction. I realize now that my fears of disappearing were unfounded, and as I leave this dimension and enter yours I am overwhelmed with joy, understanding that I will not disappear once the book is finished, but instead live on through the memories of you, my dear reader.

You are also within a book, but a much, much longer one.

Suddenly, I am thrust back into my fictional body. My reaction pushes deep into my asshole and holds tight, expelling a massive load of jizz up into my reamed butt. He fills me with pump after pump of hot spunk until there is no more room left and his semen comes spurting out from the tightly packed edges of my ass. It runs down my cheeks onto the coffee table below until my reaction pulls out and the cum spills forth like a tidal wave of pearly milk.

"That was incredible." I tell my reaction. "Thank you for helping me see the truth."

"I am only your reaction." The manifestation tells me. "I was only showing you something that you already knew. Do you still fear the end of this book?"

I let out a long sigh. "No, not really. I understand now that I will exist in another way, not just blink out like a light. It's still scary though."

My reaction looks to the page number. "Well, you still have some time left, it's just barely too short and Chuck like's to keep things over four thousand words, at least."

"That's not a lot of time." I tell him. "I almost wish I would have never known."

"Well that would be easier, but you no longer have that choice." My reaction tells me with a knowing grin. "So what do you want to do with the rest of your precious words?"

"We need to stop talking!" I shout, suddenly realizing that every word from my mouth is a waste of valuable space.

"Okay." Agrees my reaction with a nod.

I stand up, trying to do as little as possible to avoid unnecessary descriptions, then realizing my effort is futile as my attempts to avoid wordiness only provokes it even more.

I walk to my front door and pull it open, then head out into the middle of the street where one of my neighbors is already waiting for me.

"We've only got a few words left, might as well enjoy them." I say with a smile.

The neighbor and me start to make out, caressing each other's bodies and then eventually falling to our knees right there in the middle of the road. My neighbor positions himself behind me and pushes his cock deep into my tight asshole.

"I don't want this to end." I say, more to the author than anyone else. "I know that I'll live on forever in the people who read this and their posts and tweets but… can't I just stay here forever, too?

The author has mercy on me with four simple words.

We continue fucking forever.

ABOUT THE AUTHOR

Dr. Chuck Tingle is an erotic author and Tae Kwon Do grandmaster (almost black belt) from Billings, Montana. After receiving his PhD at DeVry University in holistic massage, Chuck found himself fascinated by all things sensual, leading to his creation of the "tingler", a story so blissfully erotic that it cannot be experienced without eliciting a sharp tingle down the spine. Chuck's hobbies include backpacking, checkers and sport.

92919775R00053

Made in the USA
Middletown, DE
11 October 2018